"No Way. You're Not Having A Baby. Not Here. Not Now. Not With Me!"

For the space of one endless second she continued to look at him incredulously. Then she abruptly crossed her arms above her rounded middle. Her mouth—soft, lush, with an undeniable carnality that was all wrong on an expectant mother—flattened dangerously. "All right."

It was the very last thing Jack expected. "Good" was all he could say.

"Well, thanks for the ride." She shoved open his car door and climbed out.

Jack gaped. "Where do you think you're going?"

"To get someone else to help me."

What had he ever done to deserve this? One small good deed, one humanitarian, be-a-good-citizen gesture, and suddenly he was stuck with a stubborn, unreasonable, overly independent woman who didn't have the sense to stay out of a snowstorm. A woman who, if she really was in labor, was going to have to rely on *him* to deliver her baby!

Dear Reader,

A book from Joan Hohl is always a delight, so I'm thrilled that this month we have her latest MAN OF THE MONTH, *A Memorable Man*. Naturally, this story is chock-full of Joan's trademark sensuality *and* it's got some wonderful plot twists that are sure to please you!

Also this month, Cindy Gerard's latest in her NORTHERN LIGHTS BRIDES series, *A Bride for Crimson Falls*, and Beverly Barton's "Southern sizzle" is highlighted in *A Child of Her Own*. Anne Eames has the wonderful ability to combine sensuality and humor, and *A Marriage Made in Joeville* features this talent.

The Baby Blizzard by Caroline Cross is sure to melt your heart this month—it's an extraordinary love story with a hero and heroine you'll never forget! And the month is completed with a sexy romp by Diana Mars, *Matchmaking Mona*.

In months to come, look for spectacular Silhouette Desire books by Diana Palmer, Jennifer Greene, Lass Small and many other fantastic Desire stars! And I'm always here to listen to your thoughts and opinions about the books. You can write to me at the address below.

Enjoy! I wish you hours of happy reading!

Lucia Macro

Lucia Macro
Senior Editor

Please address questions and book requests to:
Silhouette Reader Service
U.S.: 3010 Walden Ave., P.O. Box 1325, Buffalo, NY 14269
Canadian: P.O. Box 609, Fort Erie, Ont. L2A 5X3

CAROLINE CROSS
THE BABY BLIZZARD

SILHOUETTE *Desire*

Published by Silhouette Books

America's Publisher of Contemporary Romance

SILHOUETTE BOOKS

ISBN 0-373-76079-5

THE BABY BLIZZARD

Books by Caroline Cross

Silhouette Desire

Dangerous #810
Rafferty's Angel #851
Truth or Dare #910
Operation Mommy #939
Gavin's Child #1013
The Baby Blizzard #1079

CAROLINE CROSS

always loved to read, but it wasn't until she discovered
the romance genre that she felt compelled to write, fascinated by the chance to explore the positive power of
love in people's lives. Nominated for a number of
awards, including the prestigious RITA, she's been
thrilled to win the *Romantic Times* Reviewer's Choice
Award for Best Desire, as well as a W.I.S.H. Award.
She grew up in central Washington State, attended the
University of Puget Sound and now lives outside
Seattle, where she *tries to* work at home despite the
chaos created by two telephone-addicted teenage
daughters and a husband with a fondness for home-
improvement projects. Caroline would love to hear
from her readers. She can be reached at P.O. Box
5845, Bellevue, Washington, 98006.

One

By the time the pale blue Cadillac began its horrifying slide across the snow-shrouded road, Jack had been trailing behind it for several hours.

It had passed him first on the highway north of Casper. Although it was hard to believe now, when he had to fight the roaring wind and blowing snow to keep his big four-wheel-drive pickup on the road, Jack had been bored at the time. He'd been bored with the unchanging grayness of the sky, the unseasonably mild temperature, the desolate sameness of the surrounding plains.

It had seemed an oppressively dull January day.

It was that very dullness—and its failure to distract him from the black mood he'd been unable to shake since seeing Jared and Elise at the lawyer's office—that had made him take note of the Cadillac.

Plain and simple, he'd been looking for a diversion.

What he'd received instead was a blow to the armor of his indifference.

He scowled, adjusted his grip on the steering wheel as the wind buffeted the truck, and admitted he just didn't get it. So what if the Caddy's driver was a woman? That didn't explain why something as meaningless as the glance they'd exchanged the first time she passed him should affect him like a punch to the belly.

Hell, she wasn't even pretty. Striking, maybe, with that mane of hair the exact same color as his favorite sorrel mare and the sort of lush, full mouth that put a man in mind of all sorts of sinful things.

But not pretty.

Except maybe...when she smiled.

Which she had, he recalled irritably. She'd smiled straight at him, all *Mona Lisa*-knowing, when he drove past the filling station in Kaycee where she'd stopped to gas up. Just the memory set his teeth on edge. Clearly, she'd misunderstood his reason for slowing, assuming it was so he could take a second look at her. In truth, he'd merely been trying to get a bead on the weather, since it had started to snow.

Now, he narrowed his eyes against the river of white beating against the windshield. Grudgingly he conceded that—although his view of his fellow traveler had been partially blocked by an open car door—for once reality had lived up to the initial advertising. A man would have to be blind not to have noticed that her legs were long and slim, her arms and shoulders willowy, her provocative mouth balanced by a stubborn chin and dark, intelligent eyes. Just as he'd have to be obtuse not to conclude from the way the gas jockey had been scurrying around to do her bidding that the parts he couldn't see were as compelling as those he could.

So okay. For a woman who wasn't pretty, she'd been something to see with that soft, amused smile on her face and all that shiny hair blowing in the rising breeze.

Not that he cared, of course—except in the most elemental way.

Jared and Elise had seen to that. Between them, they'd cured him of caring about much of anything. Just as they'd relieved him of all his pretty ideals, his Pollyanna view of the world, his foolish hopes and secret dreams.

Maybe that was why the discovery that his libido wasn't dead after all was such a shock. For three years, since the humiliating day in the judge's chambers when he'd learned just how big a fool he really was, he'd divorced himself from intimacy. He'd banished *want* and *need* from his vocabulary. And he hadn't felt a twinge of desire—for anything or anyone.

Until today.

Jack gave a snort of disgust and wondered what had come over him. There was a whale of difference between viable lust, where you had an actual acquaintance with the person you hankered to touch, and some pointless fantasy about a total stranger. That's why it was so galling to have to admit that ever since the stranger in question had overtaken him again at Crazy Woman Creek—and had the salt to wave as she whipped past—he'd found himself wondering all sorts of things.

Such as whether that russet-colored hair was natural or not. And if her wide, full-lipped mouth would taste tart, like cherries, or as sweet as ripe berries. And how it would feel to have those long, luscious legs wrapped tightly around his waist.

And whether she made a habit of smiling at just anyone. Foolish. Simply acknowledging such thoughts was enough to make the tops of his ears feel hot. Particularly when there were far more important matters to be pondered.

For example: Where exactly did she think she was going? He'd assumed she was headed for Gillette until an hour ago, when she'd gone north at Buffalo. Then he'd guessed she must have friends or family in the tiny town of Gweneth, until she drove straight past the turnoff. He'd been hanging back, puzzling over that, when she'd stunned him by slowing down and turning onto Johnson County Road Number 9.

That was when he'd decided she was either lost or crazy or both. Because other than the Double D, which they'd passed some twenty minutes back, the only ranch for the next forty miles was his. And he knew damn well she wasn't coming to see him. Except for business, nobody came to see him anymore.

Not since he'd given away his son.

The familiar anguish splintered through him. Ruthlessly, he forced it away, reminding himself that it was over and done. It was then that the Cadillac began its inexorable slide across the road.

Jack watched in disbelief as the vehicle drifted sideways through the heavily blowing snow, spun slowly around in a heart-stopping three-hundred-and-sixty-degree turn, then disappeared from sight as if sucked into a black hole.

Instantly he eased up on the accelerator. There was no question of driving on. Jared had always claimed he was a Boy Scout at heart and, as Jack had been bitterly reminded in Casper again today, old habits died hard.

But he wasn't going to think about that now. It was over, done, past. He was alone, irrevocably on his own. Or would be, as soon as he made sure the Cadillac's driver was okay.

The thought brought him up short. Dismay splintered through him. Hell. He was actually going to have to meet this woman. *Leave it to you, Sheridan. You can't even enjoy a little red-blooded, from-a-safe-distance fantasy without reality screwing it up.*

In the very next second, he clamped down on his wayward emotions. This wasn't about him, he reminded himself harshly. This was about someone in trouble, someone in need of help. At the very best, she was going to be bruised and shaken, distraught about what had happened. And at the very worst—

Jack shoved the idea away. It was bad enough he had to get involved at all. No matter what condition this woman was in, he wasn't going to let himself care on a personal level. He'd do what he could to help, one stranger helping another, but that was it.

That was how it had to be.

Keeping an eye on the dim outline of the fence that marched along the road to his left, he let the truck roll to a stop and took a long look around.

Nothing. He could see nothing but swirling sheets of snow reflected in the beams of his headlights. He let loose a single scathing curse. Shifting the transmission into park, he pulled on the emergency brake and doused the lights. He squeezed his eyes shut, allowed them a moment's rest from the eerie onslaught of white, then slowly opened them and surveyed the area.

There. Ahead, and down a long, shallow slope to his right, was a gleam of red. He released a breath as he identified it as a taillight. Now that he knew where to look, he could see the rest of the Cadillac, too. It was barely visible, resting at an angle, with the wheels on the passenger side sunk into the shallow creekbed that paralleled the road. Snow, driven by the howling wind, was already starting to pile against the hood and windshield. The car's pale blue paint blended perfectly with the monochromatic landscape.

His heart gave a twist. In another few minutes, with twilight graying swiftly to night, he never would have seen it.

He switched the headlights back on, then reached around and grabbed the coil of nylon rope and the heavy-duty flashlight he kept behind the seat. He shrugged into his sheepskin-lined coat, flipped up the collar and jammed his Stetson more securely on his head.

After a moment's consideration, he elected to leave the truck running as a hedge against the cold. That decided, he hefted the flashlight, shoved open the door and plunged into the heart of the storm.

She was not going to panic, Tess Danielson told herself firmly.

Okay, so she'd had a little accident. On a remote, not-so-well-traveled road. In the middle of nowhere. During what was distinctly starting to look like a blizzard.

While she was willing to concede that the situation didn't look good, she was not going to give in to the dread skating along her spine.

Although...a nice loud scream might make her feel better.

A smile curled through her. Slowly, she let loose the breath she hadn't known she was holding and forced herself to breathe deeply and evenly. Things couldn't be too bad if she still had a sense of humor. Well, they could; as a Wyoming native, she'd grown up on tales of hapless motorists who got caught in this kind of weather and weren't found until the first spring thaw.

But that wasn't going to happen to her.

She refused to let it. She hadn't spent twenty-nine years bending the world to her will to give up now when it really mattered. Not when she'd only recently come to understand what was really important. Not when there were still so many things she wanted to experience. And not when she had someone else—she glanced protectively down at the ripe curve of her belly—depending on her.

She tugged on her seat belt, frowning when the buckle refused to budge. Stymied, she sat there and reconsidered that scream, but only for a second. The first thing she'd done once the car came to rest was turn off the engine. Already the air around her was starting to turn frosty. While that was better than risking carbon monoxide poisoning from a blocked or bent exhaust pipe, it was still far too cold for useless gestures.

She reached over, snagged her oversize down parka from the passenger seat and draped it around her.

And told herself—again—not to panic.

After all, she wasn't going to freeze to death in the next few minutes. If worse came to worst, she'd simply find her handbag, grab her nail scissors and hack her way through the belt.

If the scissors were there to grab.

Tess resolutely raised her chin and told herself she was not going to worry about that, either. She had an ace in the hole, she reminded herself, recalling the big, fierce-looking cowboy with whom she'd been playing car tag for the past several hours. He hadn't been that far behind her. He must have seen what had happened. More than likely, he was on his way to help her at this very moment.

Unless his heart turned out to be as black as his expression and he simply drove on.

Tess gave herself a shake. *Knock it off. This is Wyoming, remember? Not L.A. or New York. Around here, people look out for each other. He'll stop. So he looks a tad forbidding. He'll probably turn out to be reserved or shy, a real cupcake of a guy—*

"Ma'am?" came a forceful baritone shout.

A light flashed through the window. Momentarily blinded, Tess brought up her hand as the car door was unceremoniously wrenched open.

"Are you okay?" Her rescuer had to holler to be heard over a sudden roar of wind. Even so, his voice was distinct—dark and demanding. A perfect match for his face, Tess decided, as she stared at him in the faint illumination of the dome light.

Forget shy. Forget reserved. Forget cupcake.

Think intense. Think guarded. Think formidable. From what she could see beneath his hat—shadowed eyes, a straight blade of a nose, a slash of cheekbones, an imperious mouth—he was even more forbidding up close than he'd been from a distance.

"Are you hurt? *Answer me.*"

Intimidating or not, she'd never been so glad to see anyone in her life. Relief slammed into her, making moisture sting her eyes and her voice catch in her throat. She swallowed hard, suspecting as she looked up at that uncompromising face that he'd hate it if she burst into tears. She knew for a fact *she* would. She swallowed again and tried gamely for a lightness she didn't feel. "It's about time you got here."

He froze in the act of hunkering down. His eyes, pale green in the murky light, narrowed. "What?"

Forget a sense of humor, too. Tess raised her voice. "I'm fine."

He continued to stare, as if he didn't believe her. "Are you sure?"

She considered the dull ache in her lower back, concluded the pain scored no more than a two on a scale of one to ten, and opted to ignore it. "Yes."

"All right, then." Relief lightened his face, but did nothing to soften its angular planes. "Give me your hand and let's get you out of there. This storm's getting worse by the minute.''

She shook her head. "The seat belt is jammed. I can't get it unfastened.''

His eyes flickered over her jacket-covered body. Inexplicably, his jaw bunched for an instant before his expression smoothed out. He hooked the flashlight to his belt, twisted sideways so that he faced her, leaned close and reached around her. His forearm, hard and warm even through the padding of his heavy coat, brushed against the mound of her belly. "What the—?" He went very still. "What is that?"

Tess stiffened. "What's what?"

"That…lump.''

She stared at him in disbelief, oddly aware of the weight of his arm against her. "That's not a lump," she informed him. "That's me. I'm pregnant.''

He gave her a long, blank look, then snatched away his hand and rocked back on his heels. "Well, hell," he muttered, looking away. "It figures.''

The words, clearly not meant for her ears, carried with crystal clarity during a momentary lull in the wind. She raised an eyebrow. "Excuse me?''

For one long second, he remained silent, the hard line of his mouth even harder now. Then he shook his head and gave the slightest shrug. "Forget it," he murmured. He leaned forward and once more reached around her, and an instant later the belt gave way. He ducked back as if he couldn't get away fast enough. "Come on." His voice gruff, he stood.

She stayed where she was. "But the car—"

"Isn't going anywhere. Not now. Probably not for a while. Even if I could see to winch you out, the road's too icy to get any traction. In case you haven't noticed, it's dark—and getting darker."

Tess looked around in surprise. He was right. As incredible as it seemed, with the snow falling and the wind roaring, she'd been so intent on him, so totally taken with their exchange, she'd actually forgotten about the weather.

Which appeared to be getting worse. And still she hesitated. "I don't even know your name."

"Oh, for—" Annoyance flashed in those leaf-green eyes before he quickly got himself under control. "Jack," he said flatly. "My name is Jack Sheridan, okay?"

"And I'm Tess—"

"Terrific. So listen, *Tess.* We need to get to my truck. Now. While we still can."

He was right, of course. Annoyed at herself for behaving so foolishly, Tess swung her feet to the ground, trying to figure out why she felt compelled to challenge him.

The answer came a moment later, as she began the awkward process of extricating the rest of herself from the car. Without warning, Jack leaned in, grasped her firmly above each elbow and lifted her out. Then, in a few brusque, capable movements, he bundled her into her parka, zipped it, reached into the car and retrieved her car keys, pocketbook and overnight bag. "Here." He handed her the first two items. "Put your keys away and sling the shoulder strap of your purse around your neck so your hands are free, okay?"

That's when Tess knew. She'd never done very well with authority figures, and this guy was more than a little bossy. He was autocratic.

Which was a pretty petty concern, she chided herself a second later, when the wind nearly knocked her off her feet and he immediately leaped forward to steady her. Holding her firmly against his broad, hard chest, he turned to block her from the wind. "You okay?"

She lifted her chin and nodded, surprised to find that his face was several inches above hers. She was tall herself, and it wasn't often she had to look up at anyone. For a heartbeat, they stared at each other. His eyes really were the most extraordinary color—

"Shoot." He uttered the sibilant word with such disgust it sounded like an expletive. "What the hell is your husband thinking, letting you run around like this in your condition?"

It wasn't a question, and Tess knew it. For some reason, she wanted to answer him, however. "I'm not married." She had just enough presence of mind not to add that if she was, it wouldn't be to anyone who thought in terms of "letting her" do anything.

"Forget it," he replied, in what she was starting to recognize as his stock answer in awkward moments. "I've got a line running to the truck," he went on, all business again. "All you need to do is stay close to me and we shouldn't have any problems. When I turn around, I want you to put your hands under my coat and grab on to the back of my belt. Whatever you do, don't let go. Understand?"

Tess didn't need to be told twice. The driving snow stung her face and brought tears to her eyes, while the cold was so bitter it hurt to breathe. "Got it."

He searched her face. Satisfied with whatever he saw there, he finally gave a curt nod. "Good."

He turned and picked up her overnight bag as if it weighed nothing, then held his ground as she ran her hands up the backs of his denim-clad thighs and over the hard curve of his small masculine behind. Beneath the heavy coat, his cotton-clad back felt firm and solid. Heat rolled off him like a furnace. She took a half step closer and curled her fingers around his belt.

He set off, adjusting his step to her shorter stride. She held on tight, her universe condensed to the broad back in front of her, and concentrated on putting one foot in front of the other. It was no mean feat, given the sloping, uneven ground and the clumps of frozen bunchgrass that kept trying to trip her up.

Although the entire trip probably didn't last much more than a few minutes, to Tess it seemed to take forever. Accustomed to being fit, she'd found the change in her center of gravity in the past few months exasperating. Now, she gritted her teeth, frustrated by her own helplessness as she repeatedly stumbled and slipped. In several instances it was only her rescuer's iron strength that kept her upright. By the time they reached the truck, her lungs burned, the pain in her back was a solid six, and her face felt frozen.

"You okay?" Jack asked as he tossed her bag into the pickup's bed before he yanked open the door.

"Sure," she lied, leaning wearily against the wheel well. Out of breath, she mentally apologized to him for her earlier intolerance.

"Good."

He'd lost his hat. He looked younger without it. His windblown hair was dark and thick, as glossy as a child's. For some reason, that bothered her. Before she could decide why, he stepped over and dusted the snow from her head and shoulders with his gloved hands. Then he lifted her up, swung her around and deposited her on the car seat, where he brushed off her pant legs, stripped off her snow-caked boots and tossed them, the rope and the flashlight into the narrow storage area behind the seat. "Scoot over," he instructed. Stamping his own booted feet, he yanked off his gloves, shrugged out of his coat and climbed in beside her.

Tess slid over to give him more room, steeling herself against the pain squeezing her back. The well-insulated cab seemed hushed after the din outside. It was also pleasantly warm. In contrast, Tess felt chilled to the bone. She began to shiver, her teeth chattering like maracas.

Something that might have been compassion flared briefly in Jack's pale eyes. He turned up the heater fan, retrieved his coat from the back of the seat and tucked it around her. "That better?"

She nodded, incapable of speech.

That appeared to suit him just fine. Mouth set once again in a grim line, he pulled her shoulder harness around her and buckled it. Then he secured his own, released the brake and put the truck in gear. It rolled forward, fishtailing a little before the tires caught.

Tess pulled his coat tighter around her, burying her face in the soft shearling collar. The distinctive scent of horses and damp leather, familiar from her childhood, tickled her nose. Oddly comforted, she leaned back and closed her eyes.

She wasn't sure how much time passed, but eventually she began to feel less like a Popsicle and more like a person. She stretched, sighing with pleasure at the stream of hot air from the heater that blew over her stocking toes as she tried to find a position that would alleviate the persistent pain in her back.

She wound up canted sideways, toward her companion. Veiling her gaze with her lashes, she covertly studied him. She had to admit she was a little intimidated by his continuing silence. Her reaction surprised her. She'd grown up around cowboys, and she was no stranger to private, taciturn men.

Jack didn't seem to be thinking so much as brooding, however. And that tight look on his face was hardly benign.

In point of fact, he had the air of an individual who kept to himself not because he preferred his own company, but because he didn't trust anyone else's.

And yet...he *had* come to her rescue. And for all his brusque manner, his hard-fingered hands had been carefully gentle every single time he touched her.

More to the point, what did it matter? Soon they would both go their own ways, never to clap eyes on each other again—

"Didn't anyone ever teach you it's rude to stare?" Jack asked abruptly.

Tess started, then forced herself to relax, the willful part of her nature asserting itself. It was one thing to privately confess that she found him intimidating. Letting him know was something else entirely. "You're right," she said calmly. "Sorry."

"You want to explain what you're doing out here?"

Why, she wondered, did he have to be so abrupt? "Visiting my grandmother."

"Ah." He imbued the single syllable with a wealth of disdain. "But instead you got lost."

"I wasn't lost. I missed my turn."

"Right." He didn't sound as if he thought much of that, either. "I don't suppose it occurred to you when the snow started to fall that maybe you were out of your league?"

"I grew up here," she said patiently. "I know about snow."

"Huh. Could have fooled me."

"For your information, the only reason I had a problem was because I slowed down to let you pass, so I could turn around."

He snorted. "Because you were lost."

If he was trying to annoy her, he was doing a good job. "What about you?"

"What about me?"

"I suppose it's all right for you to be out in a blizzard?"

That granite face didn't change. "Damn straight. I've got heavy-duty snow tires, four-wheel drive, and I know what I'm doing. Besides, I've got obligations. If I don't get home, my stock won't get fed."

"Where's home?" She was certain he hadn't lived around here when she was a teenager. She'd remember.

"Cross Creek Ranch. We should be there in another few minutes."

Tess made no effort to hide her surprise. "Oh. But—"

"Look," he said sharply. "I'm not wild about taking you there, either. But we need to get in out of this storm while we still can, and mine's the closest place for miles."

Tess let a moment of silence pass. "Are you finished?" she asked finally.

His jaw bunched. "Yeah."

"Good. For the record, going to your place is fine. It's extremely nice of you to offer, and I appreciate it. I appreciate everything you've done."

"But—?" He kept his gaze glued to the road as he carefully braked to make a wide left turn, the headlights flashing across a sign that bore the ranch's name above a stylized carving of a rocking horse.

"When I lived here, this ranch was owned by some people named Langston."

He shot her a sharp glance as they rumbled across a cattle guard marked at both sides with orange reflectors. Around them, the landscape was hard to make out. The few trees and low-rising hills were nothing more than a series of ebony shadows against a charcoal night shrouded with blowing snow.

He slowed even more as their ride grew bumpier over the graveled drive. "You really used to live around here?"

She sighed at his obvious skepticism. "Yes. At the Double D. Mary Danielson's my grandmother." That earned her a single sharp look. "I can't figure out how I missed the turn for the driveway."

He was silent. He shifted the automatic transmission into low as the truck slid on a shallow grade. "Maybe," he said finally, "you weren't looking in the right place."

She waited for him to say more. When he didn't, she had to swallow another sigh. "Do you think you could explain that?"

He shrugged. "Your grandma cut a new road a few years back, when she had to redrill the well at Shell Butte. That must've been right after I bought out Langston, and that's been—" he shifted the truck back into regular drive "—seven years ago."

"Oh." Even though there was no way she could have known, she felt foolish. Perhaps that was why she was less than enthralled with his next comment.

"Too bad you don't bother to come home more often."

She frowned, taken aback by his obvious disapproval. "I don't think that's any of your business."

"Yeah? Well, it is when I'm stuck with you."

"Trust me. Just as soon as the storm passes, someone from the Double D will be over to get me."

He gave her another narrow look. "Your grandma left three days ago for an extended vacation."

"What?" She felt momentarily disoriented, the way she had when her car began to slide.

"It's one of those things you'd know about if you kept in touch—or were here because you'd been invited."

She bit off the instant retort that trembled on her lips. She'd be darned if she'd justify her behavior to him. She wasn't about to explain that she'd both written and called ahead, stating her intention to visit and supplying the date of her arrival. Or that her grandmother's departure was the older woman's oblique reply, an apparent payback for Tess's own decision to leave ten years ago.

For one thing, she didn't go around explaining her behavior to rude, disapproving strangers—no matter how compelling they were.

For another, unless she was mistaken, she had a much more pressing problem.

"Damn," Jack said abruptly.

"What's the matter?"

"The power's out."

Following his gaze, she glanced around as they drove into the ranch yard. Although a pair of dogs had come to attention on the back porch, not a single light glowed in welcome. Not from the pitch-roofed barn with its adjacent corrals, or the covered arena, or the rambling two-story house that looked pretty much the way she remembered it from childhood.

Tess's heart sank as she realized something more. She wasn't in the city anymore. Way out here, when the power went, so did the phones, since the two lines shared the same poles.

The icing on the cake. She took a deep breath. "Jack?"

"What?"

"Do you have a wife?"

He stared straight ahead. "Not anymore. Why? You thinking of applying for the job?"

"No." Tess shook her head, clenching her hands as the pain, previously limited to her lower back, snaked along her sides and wrapped around her middle like an invisible boa constrictor. She gave an involuntary gasp as the painful pressure increased. "I'm in labor."

Two

Jack didn't think. He reacted. *"No."* He swiveled toward Tess and shook his head. "Absolutely *not.*"

Her eyes, big and velvety like winter pansies, widened in astonishment. "What?"

"No way." He shook his head again, adamant. "You're not having a baby. Not here. Not now. *Not with me.*"

For the space of one endless, protracted second, she continued to send him that same incredulous look. Then she abruptly crossed her arms above her rounded middle and shifted her gaze to the darkness beyond the windshield. Her mouth—soft, lush, with an undeniable carnality that was all wrong on an expectant mother—flattened dangerously. "All right."

It was the very last thing he expected. Primed for an argument, he stared blankly at her, struggling to get himself under control. "Good." He knew he was behaving badly.

He told himself he didn't care. It was better than having her suspect the anxiety her announcement had brought him.

"Here." She laid his coat down on the section of seat between them. "Thanks for the loan." She shoved open the door and climbed out.

Jack gaped. "Where do you think you're going?"

"To the house. There must be someone there who'll help." She slammed the door.

Stunned, he sat frozen in place, his thoughts churning. Hell! What had he ever done to deserve this? One small good deed, one humanitarian be-a-good-citizen gesture, and suddenly he was stuck with a stubborn, unreasonable, overly independent woman who didn't have the sense to stay out of a snowstorm. A woman who, if she really was in labor, was going to have to rely on *him* to deliver her baby.

Just the idea made his throat tighten. Memories, ruthlessly suppressed for the past three years, flashed through his mind. He recalled how happy he'd been when Elise told him she was pregnant. It had been enough to make him ignore his uneasiness when she asked him to move into a spare room so that he wouldn't disturb her rest. It had sustained him through his loneliness when she insisted on moving into Gweneth her last trimester to be closer to the doctor. It had even made it possible for him to swallow his desperate disappointment when he arrived too late for the birth because someone had forgotten to call him. It had all seemed worth it when he finally held his small, precious, perfect son.

Unbidden, an arrow of longing pierced him. The boy would be almost three and a half now, walking, talking, his big green eyes full of questions—

All of sudden Jack realized what he was doing. This wasn't going to help anyone, he thought savagely, slamming a door on the past. He could rail against fate, he could rehash history, he could sit around feeling sorry for himself indefinitely, but the end result would be the same. The child was gone, forever beyond his reach...and Tess had no one to rely on but him.

He took a calming breath and forced himself to look at the situation dispassionately. Tess's labor had just started. Chances were, her baby wouldn't be born for hours, possibly not even until sometime tomorrow. Hell, by the time she was actually ready to deliver, the weather might well have improved, the phone lines might be restored and he could call for help. Once he did, she would no longer be his problem.

In the meantime, all he had to do was provide shelter and a cursory moral support. As long as they both remained calm, there was no reason why they couldn't get through this like the pair of adults they were. Unless something happened to her, he thought suddenly, as a particularly vicious gust of wind rattled the truck. For example, if she were to slip and fall...

He twisted around to grab his hat, forgetting he'd lost it, and that was when he noticed Tess's damp boots, lying exactly were he'd tossed them earlier.

Damn, damn, *damn.* The little fool was out there without any shoes! His newfound calm evaporated in a flash. He shoved open his door and scrambled out of the truck. Heedless of the fact that he'd forgotten his coat, he stormed across the yard, catching up with her in a few furious strides. Ignoring her cry of surprise, he scooped her into his arms. "You just don't learn, do you?" he shouted over the shriek of the wind.

"Learn what?" she replied, her voice muffled as she buried her face against the warmth of his thinly covered shoulder.

"To get the lay of the land before you go hightailing off." He marched up the three wide, shallow steps and across the wraparound porch, skirting a trio of wooden rockers that swayed in the breeze as if filled with invisible occupants.

"What do you mean?"

"I mean there's nobody here but me and you!" With a curt command to the dogs to stay down, he thrust open the back door, strode across the mudroom and opened the second door into the big country kitchen.

"What?" For the first time, she sounded uncertain. "What are you talking about? This is a big ranch. You can't possibly..." Her voice trailed off. She cleared her throat. "You can't possibly run it by yourself."

"The hell I can't," he said curtly. "I got rid of my herd a few years ago." His voice, though hardly more than a murmur, sounded harsh and loud in the pitch-dark quiet, but at least he'd managed to state the facts with none of the furious anguish he'd felt at the time. "Now I've just got horses."

Tess, still clutched in his arms, shifted. "Oh," she said in surprise.

Her scent came up at him, delicate, mysterious, feminine. He had a sudden, vivid recollection of how it felt to lie naked with a woman, to touch her in all her soft, silky places—

What was he thinking? She was about to have a baby. Disgusted with himself, he set her on her feet. "Stay here while I get a light. I don't want you banging into something." Despite his terse tone, he took an extra second to steady her, then strode to the big walk-in pantry, grateful for the privacy.

He halted before the shelves where the emergency supplies were kept, wondering what was the matter with him.

Three years of living like a monk, and the first time he felt so much as an itch for a woman, she happened to be pregnant by somebody else.

The irony of it sent a bitter smile twisting across his lips—and cooled his treacherous hormones like a plunge into a snowbank. With an impatient jerk, he lifted down two of the half-dozen battery-operated lanterns and thumbed on the switches. There was a dim glow and then a flash as the fluorescent bulbs came on.

He walked back into the kitchen to find Tess standing rigidly, her face pale, her mouth taut with pain. It didn't take a genius to figure out she was having a contraction. He slapped the lanterns on the kitchen table with a clatter, yanked out a chair and strode to her side. "Come on," he said gruffly. "You'd better sit down." He slung an arm around her and tried to usher her toward the chair.

"No." Stubbornly, she held her ground. "Standing… standing is better than sitting and this is…the pain is starting to fade." Another few seconds passed, and then she abruptly relaxed. Her breath sighed out and she leaned against him. After a moment, she straightened. "Thanks. I'm okay now."

Jack was damn glad somebody was. To his disgust, his heart was pounding.

He willed it to slow, watching as she took a quick look around, her eyes widening with surprise when she saw the ultra-modern kitchen with its pale birch cabinets and new appliances. An open counter was all that separated it from the family room, which was dominated by a big flagstone fireplace. The service stairs climbed the far wall, while straight ahead was the hallway that led to the living room, dining room, bathroom and den, and the more formal main staircase.

In the family room, there was a couch and a pair of

overstuffed chairs atop a dark area rug, the varying gray, green and cream fabrics bled of color by the room's deep shadows. A built-in entertainment center occupied the wall to the right of the fireplace, notable for the large empty space where the TV should have been.

Jack wondered what his guest would say if he told her he'd smashed it into a thousand pieces the night his wife announced she was leaving him.

Not that it was any of her business. "How far apart are the pains?"

"I'm not sure," she said unsteadily. "Maybe...four minutes?"

"Four minutes?" He loosened his grip and stepped back as if she'd goosed him. "What are you talking about? I thought they just started."

She shrugged. "Actually, my back has hurt off and on since this morning. I just didn't realize what it was."

So much for calling for help tomorrow. He took a hard, critical look at her midsection. Elise, though a full head shorter, had been twice that size when she delivered. "How far along are you?"

"Eight and a half months."

Part of him relaxed; the baby should be all right. But part of him was unexpectedly furious, stunned by her irresponsibility. "What the hell were you thinking, running around the countryside when you're this far along?" he demanded.

A wash of color rose in her chill-pinkened cheeks. "Listen, *Jack.* I didn't do this just to ruin your day. And despite what you seem to think, I'm not some reckless airhead. I saw my doctor yesterday. She didn't see anything to indicate I was about to deliver, and I didn't expect to get caught in a blizzard. Why should I? It wasn't predicted, and until today, this has been the mildest winter on record. However—" she took a deep breath as she struggled to control her temper "—it's also not your problem. So if you could just spare me a room, I promise not to bother you."

"Don't tempt me." Despite his words, he felt an unwanted twinge of admiration for her nerve—until he remembered how far her labor had progressed. Four minutes! Hell, she was going to need all the nerve she could scrape together and then some. He picked up the lamp and thrust it at her. "Here. Hold this."

"Why?" she started to ask, only to give a startled yelp as he swept her up in his arms.

"Because I've only got two hands." He headed for the service stairs that spanned the interior wall. "And you're not exactly a fragile flower."

"Put me down," she ordered, clutching his neck for balance.

He gave an involuntary grunt as she jabbed him in the chest with her elbow. "Forget it. Apparently you haven't noticed, but your socks are covered with snow, which means your feet are probably half-frozen. All I need to round out my day is for you to slip and fall. Now hold still before I lose my balance and break both our necks."

She gave a little huff, but quit squirming. After a moment's silence, she asked, "Where are we going?"

Didn't she ever quit talking? "Upstairs."

"Why?"

"Because it's cold. Because even with the emergency generator, it's going to take hours to get this place warmed up. Because the only room in the house with a bed, a bathroom and a fireplace—all of which you're going to need—is upstairs. Okay? Satisfied?" He gave her a quick, impatient glance. "Or is there something else you have to know? My social security number? My shirt size?"

"Look, I'm sorry—"

"Yeah, right." She couldn't be half as sorry as he was, he reflected, angling sideways to avoid knocking her into the walls that enclosed the steep, narrow risers.

But then, he'd cut out his tongue before he admitted that he hadn't set foot on the second floor more than a half dozen times in the past trio of years. Or that when he had, it had been only briefly, to fetch and haul for his mother who showed up periodically to fuss at him about getting on with his life. It was certainly none of Ms. Danielson's business that for him the upper reaches of the house teemed with memories he preferred to ignore.

It was nobody's business but his own.

He rounded the corner at the top of the stairs and made his way down the long hall to the closed double doors that marked the master suite, where he deposited Tess on her feet. Face set, he hesitated for the barest instant, then reached for the polished brass handles.

"Jack—"

Sunk in thought, he jerked his head around in surprise as she laid her hand on his shoulder. *"What?"*

"You don't have to give up your bedroom for me," she said softly. "I'll be fine somewhere else—"

Her sudden concern was worse than her questions. Alarmed at what she might have seen in his face to prompt such an offer, he shrugged off her hand and thrust open the door. "I sleep downstairs." He strode to the fireplace, hunkered down and opened the fire screen. "Hold the lamp steady, will you?"

He wondered what she'd make of the room. It was decorated in what Elise had claimed was pseudo-Victorian, but what he'd privately always termed Neo-Pretentious. A thick white rug, totally impractical for a working ranch, covered the wood floor. Lace swags hid the more practical window shades. The queen-size bed had a fussy floral bedspread and canopy, while the chairs that faced the fireplace were slipcovered in a contrasting geometric pattern. As for the rest...well, anything that didn't have a ruffle or a flounce had a fringe or a bow. The overall effect made his teeth ache.

He checked the damper, then lit the kindling beneath the logs already laid on the grate. To his relief, the fire caught immediately. He closed the screen, glanced pointedly at Tess and jerked his head toward the bed. "Sit down so I can have a look at your feet."

For a moment she didn't move, but then she walked over, set the lantern on the nightstand and sat on the mattress edge.

He knelt and peeled off her socks. Her icy feet were long and slim. "They look all right," he said after a careful inspection, relieved to find none of the telltale white spots that would indicate frostbite. "How do they feel?"

"Cold." He glanced up, surprised to see the corners of her mouth curve up in a tentative smile. "But otherwise okay. Thanks."

He shrugged. "Forget it." Her eyes weren't really blue at all, he saw, but closer to the purple color of the gentian violet he used to treat minor cuts on the livestock.

"Jack?"

"What?"

"Did you and your wife.... Do you have any children?"

He couldn't believe his ears. He stood. "That's none of your business."

"You're right," she said immediately. "I'm sorry. I just thought it might help if one of us knew what they were doing—"

"The bathroom's through there." He indicated the door set into the wall at her right. "I need to move the truck and get the generator started and check on my horses, but

I'll bring you your bag, some dry socks and some extra blankets before I go.''

"All right.''

"Do you have a watch?''

She shook her head. ''No, I'm afraid I—''

"Here.'' Cutting across her explanation, he stripped off his and handed it to her.

She clutched it in her hand. ''Thank you.''

"I'll see you in a little while.'' Face set, he strode from the room.

Tess was blessed with an iron constitution. She rarely got sick, but when she did she always bounced back in record time. She was also lucky; despite being both adventurous and athletic, and having tried everything from hang gliding to parasailing, she'd never broken a bone or suffered a serious injury.

That was probably why she was so scared now.

Standing with her hands braced against the mantelpiece, she prayed for the current contraction to ease. As silly as it seemed, she was shocked by how much being in labor hurt—and how quickly that pain was wearing her down. She couldn't seem to rise above it, or outsmart it, or brazen it out, the way she had so many other obstacles in her life. Given that things would likely get worse before they got better, she was starting to suspect that she wasn't going to make it through the next few hours with any dignity whatsoever.

It was a humbling admission. Tess considered her strength, both mental and physical, to be as much a part of her as her utterly straight hair, her too-wide mouth, her tendency to do what she felt was right, regardless of the consequences. But now, when she needed it most, her strength seemed to have deserted her. It had gone missing along with her nerve and her luck—

Stop it. Stop feeling sorry for yourself and think about something else.

Okay. How about that this wasn't even close to what she'd pictured when she envisioned giving birth? She'd wanted her and Gray's child, conceived out of such incredible sadness, to be born in tranquil, joyous circumstances. She'd even had a plan: Beethoven on the CD player in the birthing room at Eastside Hospital; her friend and obstetrician, Joanne Fetzer, in attendance; herself, in control, her life in order, ready to welcome the future after having made peace with her past.

Instead, that past, in the form of her grandmother, had lit out for God knew where. The baby was early. And she didn't have the calm, ultracompetent Dr. Fetzer to depend on. Instead, her designated stork was the ultimate charm school dropout—and an undependable one, at that. True, he'd brought her the things he'd promised. But that had been more than forty minutes ago. While Tess could practically hear her childbirth instructor prattling on about how first births usually took forever, that obviously wasn't the case here. If Jack didn't show up soon, he was going to miss the main event.

Not, she chided herself, that she was counting on him to be much help. He'd made it clear he'd prefer not to be part of the delivery. And as much as she'd have liked to hold it against him, she couldn't—not when her own mind shut down every time she tried to visualize the two of them sharing such intimacy. It would be daunting enough with someone she already knew, or with someone older or kinder or more approachable. But to even consider it with Jack... Well, the idea was simply impossible.

Although she supposed that anything would be better than being alone...

The contraction began to ease. She waited until she was sure it was over before she released her stranglehold on the mantel, and even then she didn't lift her head until she heard a faint, unfamiliar rumble. She glanced around, then realized the noise was the sound of the furnace coming on. Her heart started to pound. Moving carefully, she walked to the door and looked down the hall, and was rewarded when a light bloomed on at the base of the stairs. A moment later Jack appeared, a stack of supplies in his arms.

Finally. For the second time that night, tears of relief welled in Tess's eyes. Only this time, she was unable to will them away, and they spilled down her cheeks. Mortified, she ducked back inside and shuffled toward the fireplace, praying he hadn't seen her. Her back to the door, she barely managed to strike a casual pose when she heard him stride into the room.

His footsteps ceased. "What are you doing up?" She could hear the surprise in his voice.

Apparently his time at the barn hadn't done a thing to improve his manner. She swallowed. "I was cold," she murmured, her voice raw.

Thankfully, he didn't seem to notice. "So why aren't you in bed, under the covers?"

"My back hurts. I don't want to lie down." She certainly didn't feel compelled to explain that being upright gave her an illusion of control she wasn't ready to surrender.

"Huh."

She could feel him studying her. She pretended absorption in the fire, grateful for the flickering shadows.

"How far apart are the pains?"

"Two minutes."

"Are you sure?"

"Yes." She cleared her throat again. "What took you so long?"

"I had to feed the horses."

"Ah." Out of the corner of her eye, she saw him head toward the dresser.

"I brought some things. Towels. More sheets and blankets. Some scissors and string." Light flooded the room as he switched on a lamp.

"Ah," she said again. She wondered what he planned to do with the string. She'd just decided she didn't want to know when the familiar tightening began to spread across her middle. She bit her lip and pressed a hand to the small of her back, making a wordless little murmur of protest as the contraction rolled through her like a wave. She reached blindly for the back of the chair to one side of her, her fingers digging into the plush-covered frame until the pain began to ebb.

Gradually she grew aware of the awkward quality of the silence, unbroken except for the crackle of the wood in the fireplace and the steady wail of the wind whistling around the house. She swiped at her damp face, feeling foolish when she realized her hand was shaking.

Jack cleared his throat. "You okay?"

"Yes." She straightened and turned slowly in his direction. To her surprise, he was only a few feet away, as if he'd started toward her, then changed his mind. For a moment, their eyes met. The line of his mouth tightened, and she realized how she must look, her cheeks shiny, her nose red, her eyes puffy. She looked away.

"I brought a tarp for the mattress," he said gruffly. He took a step toward the bed, then stopped and gestured toward the thermos sharing space on the dresser with the other things he'd brought. He gestured toward the dresser. "Are you thirsty? I made some coffee."

Just the thought made her stomach roll. She shook her head. "No thanks."

"Okay." He moved to the far side of the bed, peeled back the covers and unfolded a rectangle of canvas. Determined not to dwell on the panic that threatened to overwhelm her, she focused on his hands. They were large, with long, elegant fingers, their every gesture deft, sure and competent. She supposed she ought to feel reassured.

She didn't.

As if he felt her watching him, he looked up. His gaze flickered over her. "Interesting outfit."

She fingered the sheet, folded in half and wrapped around her waist, that she was wearing in lieu of her pants. "My water broke." She couldn't resist the little devil that made her add, "Be glad you weren't here. It wasn't pretty."

He gave her a sharp glance, his hands stilling briefly before he resumed smoothing out the sheet he'd stretched over the tarp. He shook his head. "I bet you were a real pain in the butt as a kid."

She couldn't contain a slight smile. "Still am."

He flashed her another look, and she thought she detected a flicker of surprise in his leaf-green eyes. He pulled the covers back into place. "Yeah, well... I suppose you come by it honestly."

"How do you mean?"

He shrugged. "I've done business with your grandmother. She can be a little...difficult."

Tess made an unladylike sound. "Impossible is more like it. Where Gram's concerned, there's only one way to do anything—hers."

He came around the bed. She tensed as he closed the distance between them, then felt foolish as he reached past

her for the poker, squatted down and attended to the fire.
"Is that why you left? You couldn't get your own way?"

She looked down at his dark head, taking note of the
way the hair feathered over his shirt collar. "I suppose you
could say that. I wanted to go to college, see more of the
world than northern Wyoming. Gram wouldn't hear of it.
As far as she was concerned, the Double D *was* the world."

Jack tossed another log on the fire. "But you went anyway, right?" His voice had an edge she didn't understand.

"That's right." She was darned if she'd explain that
she'd written regularly, concerned that her grandmother
might worry. Or that every letter had been returned, bearing
the single word *Refused* penned in Mary's decisive handwriting. He'd obviously already reached some sort of conclusion about her character—and it wasn't pretty.

He climbed to his feet. He was so close she could see
the faint, silvery line of a scar high on his right cheekbone.
"So why show up now? Or—" he glanced pointedly down
at the taut bulge of her belly "—do I need to ask?"

She wondered again why he seemed so determined to
assume the worst. "Look. I'm not indigent, and I didn't
come here for a handout or to beg a roof over my head. I
came because I thought my grandmother ought to know
she was about to have a great-grandchild."

"Yeah? I bet the kid's father is thrilled about that," he
muttered.

It was the second time that night he'd brought up the
baby's father, and Tess had enough. "Save your sympathy," she said tersely, "at least for Gray. He's dead."

If she meant to surprise him, she'd succeeded. Although
his expression didn't change, she could see the shock in his
glorious green eyes—and an unmistakable flash of regret
for what he'd said.

All of a sudden, she felt exhausted, and more than a little

ashamed herself. She turned away, back toward the fire. "Please. Just go away— *Oh!*" She gasped as a bolt of pain lanced through her, doubling her over.

She forgot her anger at Jack as she realized that this contraction already felt far worse than the preceding ones. She gritted her teeth so hard her jaw ached, but it didn't help. Instead, the pain increased, winding tighter and tighter. Tess began to panic. She couldn't do this, she thought frantically, little black dots dancing behind her eyelids as she squeezed her eyes shut. She could handle an accident, a blizzard, Gram's rejection, Gray's loss, a hostile stranger—but not this excruciating, overwhelming, unrelenting pain, too. She swayed, biting her lip to keep from crying out, afraid that if she started, she wouldn't be able to stop.

Suddenly a hard, steely arm came around her. "Breathe," Jack ordered, his deep, impatient voice close to her ear.

Disoriented, she forced her eyes open. "What?"

He stared down at her, his expression grim. "I said *breathe*. In through your nose and out through your mouth. Like this." He demonstrated.

Gasping fitfully, she shook her head. "I— I—can't."

True to form, he disagreed. "You *can*. Look at me and concentrate."

His certainty—and some last little remnant of bravado— brought her chin up. Clutching his arm, she ignored the tears blurring her vision and attempted to pattern her breathing after his. It wasn't easy. At first she felt so frantic and light-headed that with every breath she was sure she was going to hyperventilate.

Jack wasn't having it, however. Through the sheer force of his will, he kept her focused until she was gradually able to inhale and exhale more and more deeply. At some point, the pain seemed to lessen a fraction.

Even so, an eternity seemed to pass before the contraction finally ended. Dazed, every muscle in her body quivering, Tess sagged against Jack. He felt wonderful, lean, hard, warm and solid, and she was suddenly too grateful for his presence to be concerned with anything else. "Thanks," she said when she finally found her voice.

He tensed, but didn't move away. "Why the hell didn't you take a childbirth class?"

She swallowed a sigh. *Forget cupcake—remember?* "I did. I've just never been very good at following directions."

Silence. And then a grunt. "Huh. I never would've guessed."

"What about you?"

"What about me?"

"Do you practice being rude?" she asked mildly, finally looking up at him. "Or is it a natural talent?"

Their gazes met for a long, measuring moment. Whatever he felt was impossible to decipher, but for once he was the first to look away. "Can you walk?"

"Yes. Can you?"

He shook his head. "What I meant," he said caustically, "was do you think you can make it to the bed?"

She considered. Her lower body felt leaden, the muscles weighted. "I don't know. Why?"

"Because you need to lie down before the baby shows up and drops out on its head."

She sighed, this time loudly and on purpose. "You know, Jack, you really have a way with words."

"Can you walk or not?"

It was only five feet. How hard could it be? "Sure." She let loose of him and took a step.

A second later, a new contraction struck her, and her knees gave out.

Three

"**W**hat is it with you?" Jack demanded as the contraction finally eased and Tess loosened the punishing grip she had on his hand. He sat back, shifting to a more settled position on the edge of the bed. Despite his outer calm and the deliberate way he'd coached her along, his heart was still thundering from how close she'd come to falling flat on her face. "You take an oath against asking for help?"

Tess hitched herself up higher against the pile of pillows he'd placed at her back and sent him a reproachful glance. "Gosh, Jack. Don't start being nice now or I'll really lose it."

The cheeky response tugged at him. All right. So he didn't exactly like her. She was too willful, too smart, too *here*. That didn't mean he couldn't admire her grit. "You just don't quit, do you?"

She shook her head. "No. But if it's any consolation, this isn't quite how I envisioned having this baby, either."

Their eyes met, and something inside him stilled when he saw the look in hers a second before she glanced away. Hell. If it was anyone else, he'd swear that beneath that glib exterior, she was…scared.

The idea brought him up short. As did his sudden, unsettling realization that ever since he'd yanked open the Cadillac's door all those hours ago, he'd been so provoked by her intrusion into his life and so preoccupied with how he felt about it, he'd taken her seemingly inexhaustible composure at face value. She'd acted as if she could handle anything, and he'd believed it.

Now, as if a blindfold had been ripped away, he could see the quiver at the corners of her mouth, the pulse pounding at the base of her throat, the effort behind her composure.

And he didn't like it. He didn't like it at all. "Hey," he said, more sharply than he intended. "What's the matter?" *Nice. If they were giving prizes for stupid, you'd need a trophy case.*

Thankfully, she was so busy studying the fire, she didn't seem to notice. "Nothing. It just…hurts."

He could see how much the admission cost her. "Oh." Another intelligent response. Frustrated, he searched for something relevant to say. "Yeah, well…I think you're through transition, so it shouldn't take much longer."

The instant the words left his mouth, he knew he'd made a mistake.

Her head came around. Questions suddenly crowded her eyes. How come he knew so much? Where had he come by such knowledge?

It was a measure of her ability to unsettle him that for an instant Jack was tempted to explain. Except…what the hell would he say? That once upon a time he'd had a pregnant wife? That in an effort to be a good husband, a good father, he'd learned everything he could about pregnancy and childbirth, postpartum care and infant development?

Yeah, right—and then what? *You going to tell her how, in the end, none of it mattered? You going to cry on her shoulder, tell her how Elise left you, explain why you gave up your son?*

No way.

"Jack—"

"What?" He braced, wondering what she'd ask first.

As if she sensed his imminent withdrawal, Tess reached out and entwined her fingers with his, as if to anchor some part of him in place. "Can I get that part about this...not taking much longer...in writing?"

For a moment he was sure he hadn't heard her right. Then he assumed she must be toying with him. Anger flashed through him. He jerked his gaze to her face.

To his surprise, she wasn't even looking at him. As a matter of fact, her eyes were shut, her lips pressed together. She clutched at his hand as the mound of her stomach began to tighten convulsively. "Oh!" she gasped, holding on to him for dear life. "Oh, Jack, it hurts—!"

Her trust, in the face of what he'd been thinking, brought the last line of his defenses crashing down. "Easy. It's okay—"

But it wasn't. The contraction bowed her back, brought her arching up off the bed. She opened her eyes, staring at him in helpless distress.

He felt an edge of panic, and struggled to get a grip on himself. God knew, there wasn't a whole lot he could do for her except pretend to be calm. He caught her other hand, as if to lend her some of his strength by the contact. "Stop fighting it," he said forcefully. "I know it hurts, but you're doing fine. Just don't forget to breathe."

She nodded, the flesh across her nose and cheeks taut with strain.

Then there was no more time for conversation, as the contractions began to come one after another, faster and faster. Everything seemed to blur together, the labored sound of her breathing, the muscle-wrenching expenditure of effort, the unrelenting, escalating cycle of pain. Jack didn't know how much time had passed when Tess suddenly gave a tremendous shudder. Her eyes widened. "Oh! I can't— There's something— It's coming—"

Earlier, out in the barn, he'd imagined this moment with dread. Not the mechanics of it; he'd barely given that a second thought. Like every rancher, he'd helped deliver his fair share of calves and foals, and he was more than familiar with the nuts and bolts of birth.

But to share such extreme intimacy with a stranger, especially one he found so disturbing... He'd been sure it would be awkward, uncomfortable, embarrassing for them both.

Yet, sometime in the past hour, he'd ceased to think of Tess as a stranger. As a result, he didn't even stop to think, much less hesitate. "Wait! Don't push, not yet, let me check, make sure it's all right—" Without quite knowing how he'd gotten there, he found himself kneeling in the center of the bed, his hands warm and steady against Tess's cold, bare, shaking knees. As if it were the most natural thing in the world, he looked down, saw the top of the baby's head emerging, and felt a mixture of awe and excitement spiral through him. Moisture, unexpected and mortifying, stung his eyes. He swallowed hard before he looked up at Tess. "So what are you waiting for? Push!"

From somewhere, she found the energy to roll her eyes before she pursed her lips, braced herself against the pillows and began to strain.

Once. Twice. A third time. Jack watched her struggle with a mixture of wonder and growing concern.

"Okay, okay... The head's clear... There's one shoulder...now the other... Come on...you can do it..."

"Ohhh...ohhhh..." She fell back against the pillows, breathing like a bellows. She was white-faced with exhaustion.

"Come on." He was suddenly afraid that if she stopped now, she wouldn't find the strength—or the courage—to resume. "Again."

"I'm so tired—"

"I know." As if his movements were dictated by some power outside himself, he found himself reaching up and gently brushing her hair off her face. "Listen. You can do this. But you have to concentrate."

"Right." Her mouth trembled as she tried to smile. "Wanna trade places...and see...if you still feel...the same way?"

Something alarmingly like tenderness curled through him. "No way. Now, shut up and *push*."

She opened her mouth to protest, then changed her mind, apparently seeing something in his face that convinced her he wasn't going to let up. Gritting her teeth, she dug down deep, and found some last little reserve of strength. Jaw clenched, she pushed.

Jack sat back. "That's right, that's it. Come on. You're almost there—"

She strained again, calling out. For a moment, nothing happened.

And then her cry was answered by a high, wavering baby's wail.

Stunned, Jack stared down at the squalling infant suddenly filling his hands. He felt an instant of unreality, a rush of astonishment. Swift on its heels came an explosion of elation, as bright and intoxicating as champagne.

"Tess—" for some reason, his voice was shaking "—it's a girl!"

For an instant she looked blank. "What? I thought—are you sure?"

He nodded. "Yes."

Her lips began to tremble. "Is she okay?"

"She's perfect." Quickly he toweled off the baby, wrapped her in a blanket and handed her to her mother. "Honest. Ten fingers and ten toes."

"Oh. Oh, my." Tess looked down at the little red face and managed a shaky smile. "She's...beautiful."

"Yeah." He swallowed. The damn moisture was filling his eyes again, and he seemed to have something stuck in his throat. Nevertheless, there was something he had to say. "You...you did great."

She glanced up in surprise. For a long moment, their gazes met. Until, with no warning, her face crumpled and she began to cry, great wrenching sobs of exhaustion, relief and joy.

For the second time that night, Jack didn't stop to think. He simply moved up the bed and gathered her and the baby into his arms.

Jack awoke slowly the next morning.

He was conscious first of the light. It was silvery-white against his eyelids, indicating that it was well past dawn, his usual time for rising. Perplexed, he started to stretch, only to be further disconcerted when he felt the chair at his back. Hell. Why wasn't he in bed? He rolled his head, winced at the crick in his neck—and froze as his cheek brushed against an impossibly silky little head. In nearly the same instant, he registered the soft, slight weight resting against his chest.

The baby. Memory rushed back. The storm, the accident,

Tess... And then later, the accelerated labor, the incredible moment of birth...

He raised his head and opened his eyes, forgetting to breathe as he took in Tess's daughter's serene, sleepy little face, so close to his. His gaze traced the fan of spidery black lashes that brushed the rose-petal cheeks, took in the button nose and the Cupid's-bow lips parted to form a perfect O. Beneath his hand, he could feel each delicate bump of her spine, the steady ebb and flow of her breathing, the rhythmic flutter of her heart.

An odd pain squeezed his heart. He hadn't lied last night. She *was* perfect.

For one unguarded instant, he wanted nothing more than to gather her closer, to assure her that he'd never let anyone hurt her, to tell her that he'd steady her if she stumbled and catch her if she fell. He wanted to promise that he'd be there for bee stings and skinned knees, for ponies and tea parties. That he'd see her from teddy bears to proms, from fairy tales to real-life princes, through dreams, disappointments, tears and triumphs.

And then, like a slap in the face, his reason returned. God, he was losing it. Hadn't he learned anything? What was he doing, sitting here spinning pipe dreams about another man's child? A child he knew full well would be gone in a day or two.

Which was exactly what he wanted, he was quick to remind himself. But even if it wasn't, if by some impossible twist of fate she were to stay forever, it still wouldn't matter.

He was done with things he couldn't count on. Like love. And fidelity. And caring. Heck, he was just plain done with other people, regardless of their size.

So why, he wondered, as the baby stirred, her eyelashes fluttering and her dainty mouth puckering before she settled back into sleep, did she have to be such a fetching little thing? Why couldn't she be red and wizened? Or have a pointed head? What was it about her that made him want to hold her close and make ridiculous promises he couldn't keep?

Hell. Who knew the why of anything? All he knew was that he was the same man today that he'd been yesterday. That the only thing that had changed was that yesterday this baby had yet to be born. And he had yet to meet her mother...

Tess. It was *her* fault he was feeling this way. Somehow, with her nerve and her courage and her never-say-die sense of humor, she'd managed to get to him last night, to resurrect the ghost of the man he'd been before. The one who had believed in the Golden Rule. The one who'd been naive enough to think that if you worked hard, played fair and lived right, you'd succeed at life.

Stupid. In the clear light of day, he knew better. After what he'd been through, he ought to—

"Jack?"

The soft sound of his name pinned him in place. His gaze sliced toward the bed, where he found Tess propped up on her side...watching him. His stomach rolled. There was something in her expression, a certain softness about her eyes, a tender twist to her mouth, that told him she expected him to act the way he had last night. And that she'd jumped to some silly, sentimental conclusion—like maybe she thought they were friends or something.

The sooner he set her straight, the better. "You're awake."

It sounded more like an accusation than a statement. Taken aback, Tess sat up, struggling not to show her surprise. "Yes, I am." She met Jack's gaze, trying to square the cool-eyed stranger confronting her with the strong, steady, reassuring man who'd occupied that same big lean body only hours ago.

That man had not only safely delivered her baby and comforted her afterward, but had also taken care of all the things she'd been too exhausted to. He'd matter-of-factly dealt with the umbilical cord and a host of other decidedly unglamorous cleanup chores. He'd weighed, measured, washed and diapered the baby. He'd even helped her wash her face and brush the tangles out of her hair, lent her one of his own flannel shirts to wear and made sure she had fresh sheets to sleep on. As foolish as it seemed now, in light of his guarded expression, Tess had drifted to sleep thinking, *My hero...*

Clearly, it was not a role he intended to accept. Needing a moment to think, she said mildly, "It sounds as if it's still blowing pretty hard outside." As observations went, it was hardly brilliant; the steady howl of the wind was self-evident.

Jack treated it as such and gave a dismissive shrug. "Yeah, I guess."

She scooted a little higher against the pillows, trying to ignore the strident protest of more muscles than she'd known she possessed. She nodded at the baby. "Is she all right?"

"Sure."

He said it too quickly. Puzzled by the trace of defensiveness she could hear in his voice, she glanced briefly at the beautiful pine cradle that had mysteriously materialized last night. "Then why are you holding her?"

"She was fussing earlier."

"Gosh, I'm sorry. I didn't hear her."

"Yeah, well...you were pretty tired. How do you feel, by the way?" His gaze met hers in a silent challenge.

"Me? I'm fine."

His mouth curved sardonically. "Right."

Those guarded green eyes didn't miss much. She shrugged, and sent him a disarming smile. "Okay, I confess. I feel like I was hit by a bus. Happy?" The last thing she wanted to do was argue with him. Not after all he'd done for her. And not when she found him so disturbing, with his disheveled hair, his whisker-shadowed jaw—his quiet but unmistakable withdrawal.

He nodded toward the nightstand to her right. "I thought maybe some aspirin would help."

She looked over, saw the small bottle and the glass of water. He ought to carry a warning label, she thought ruefully. *Caution: Master of the Unexpected.* "Thanks."

There was a considerable silence before diversion arrived in the form of the baby, who had the good grace to choose that particular moment to give a little start and wake up.

Almost imperceptibly Jack's expression softened. He looked down, then lifted the infant higher on his shoulder, gently patting her back in an age-old gesture of comfort. The blanket slid down, revealing the back of the baby's head. Covered in fine dark fuzz, it looked impossibly small compared to his hand. Tess's stomach suddenly felt hollow. There was something so compelling about the picture they made together, the baby so small and helpless, Jack so big, so remote, so watchful.

He climbed to his feet and started toward the bed. "Here. You'd better take her."

"Oh, but—" She opened her mouth to protest, then caught herself. Yesterday, she wouldn't have thought twice about confiding that she'd never held a baby under the age of two. But then, yesterday she hadn't given a whit what he thought of her.

Besides, she *wanted* to hold her daughter. She was simply a little nervous, afraid she'd do something wrong. "All right." Reaching up, she slid her fingers beneath Jack's. Dismissing the inexplicable tingle that danced down her spine as their hands rubbed together, she started to lift the infant away.

"Don't forget to support her head," Jack muttered.

"Oh, of course." She quickly slid one hand beneath the baby's wobbly neck before cuddling her close. "Hey, little one. Aren't you pretty?" She wasn't sure where the words came from; suddenly they were just there, trembling on her tongue. "I'm your mama." Delight curled through her as the baby locked on her voice, her dark blue eyes focusing intently on Tess's face. She touched her finger to one small hand, awed when the baby grabbed hold with an almost painfully firm grip.

"I can't believe how strong she is." She glanced up at Jack to share her amazement—and to ask about the tiny white shirt her daughter was wearing.

For once, she caught him with his normally unreadable face unguarded. His gaze was fixed on the baby; his expression was so bleak it made her heart contract.

"Jack?" She wasn't sure if she said his name out loud or merely thought it.

Whichever it was, the result was the same. He stiffened and gave her a single blank look, then abruptly turned and strode toward the farthest window.

Shaken, she stared after him. She watched as he twitched aside the curtain, yanked up the shade and stared outside. She didn't know what to say. Not that it mattered. The tense set of his shoulders forbade conversation.

And yet she couldn't forget the remarkable sense of kinship she'd felt with him last night. It made that look of anguish all the more unacceptable.

She looked down at her daughter, then back at Jack, trying to think of a way to ease the situation. "So." She

cleared her throat. "What's the weather doing out there?"
Oh, good, Tess.

For a moment, she thought he wouldn't answer. Then
she almost wished he hadn't. "Snowing," he said caustically.

"Any sign that it's going to let up?"

"What do I look like? The National Weather Service?"

So much for small talk. She cast around for another subject, but what could she say? That she owed him her baby's
life, a debt she could never repay? That even though they'd
known each other less than twenty-four hours, he meant a
lot to her? That she'd like to be his friend?

She could imagine his reaction.

As if the situation weren't already awkward enough, the
baby began to fuss, pursing her rosebud lips and making
intermittent little bleats of distress. Not knowing what else
to do, Tess shifted the child closer and tried gently rocking
her. "Shh... It's all right."

The baby stiffened. The bleats got louder.

"Shh...don't cry. It's all right," she murmured. She
stared at the infant's face, which currently resembled a miniature gargoyle's, and told herself she wasn't going to
panic. "What's the matter, sweetie?"

It was Jack who answered. "She probably thinks she's
hungry," he informed her, a trace of impatience coloring
his voice.

She glanced at him in surprise. It wasn't what he'd said
that was so startling, but *how* he'd said it—easily, automatically—the way only someone experienced with the
subject would respond. It was the same way he'd sounded
last night, when he'd coached her breathing and com-
mented on her progress through transition, she realized.

Only then, she'd been in too much pain to dwell on why
he knew so much.

Now, she wasn't.

Her gaze sought the cradle, which she suddenly saw with new eyes. Then she glanced at the baby's shirt—and that was when she realized the soft blue blanket her daughter was wrapped in wasn't any old blanket. Not only was it exactly the right weight and size for an infant, but someone had embroidered an elaborate rocking horse on the corner, just like the one she'd seen on the ranch sign when they'd driven in.

She looked over at Jack. He stared stonily back, and something about his expression—its determined blankness, its calculated lack of emotion—turned what until that moment had been mere speculation into certainty.

There'd been a child in his life in the not-too-distant past. A child whose absence still hurt him.

His next words confirmed it. "My son—" his mouth twisted with a hint of self-mockery she didn't understand "—is three and a half. He lives in Casper with his mother and stepfather."

"Oh." She tried to take it in, to understand the sudden edge to his voice. "Do you see him often?"

"No." His gaze fixed on her. "I don't see him at all." His look defied her to comment further.

Shocked by his callous statement, she tore her gaze from him to her daughter as the baby gave a sudden wail. For a second, her mind was blank, and then she realized there was actually something she could do about *this*. She breathed a sudden sigh of relief. Awkwardly cradling the little girl against her, she began to unbutton her shirt.

Across the room, Jack stiffened. "What are you doing?"

She hoped bravado would pass for confidence. "You said she was hungry. I thought I'd...nurse."

His gaze flickered to the widening gap in her shirt. His jaw suddenly bunched, and he looked back at her face, his green eyes hooded. "Good idea." Despite the words, his tone suggested it was anything but. "While you're doing that, there are some things I should take care of."

"But—"

"But what?"

There was no reason to panic, Tess chided herself. She'd traveled all over the world on her own. Surely she could manage one small baby girl. "Nothing. That's fine."

"All right, then." With a haste strangely at odds with his deliberate manner, he hightailed it out the door as if afraid she'd change her mind if he lingered.

Tess watched him go. A line of Winston Churchill's crept into her mind. The great British statesman had been contemplating Russia and had concluded that it was "a riddle, wrapped in a mystery inside an enigma."

Winston, she reflected, should have known Jack.

It took an hour of hard labor before Jack started to feel better. He pushed himself, cleaning stalls, hauling feed, carrying water, working himself into a muscle-aching sweat, until the tense, edgy feeling that had slammed into him when Tess had begun to undo her shirt receded. By the time he forked a last leaf of fresh hay into the last cleaned stall, he'd regained a semblance of control.

But he wasn't happy about it. Or even particularly relieved. He was too damn tangled up inside to even come close.

He'd thought, when he first woke up this morning, that it was only the baby who had gotten beneath his defenses. He hadn't liked it, hadn't liked the longing that twisted his guts and made him ache with the need to cherish, defend and nurture her, but he'd thought he understood it. Given the hole in his life since Elise had taken the boy, it wasn't strange that the baby, all new and innocent and defenseless, should trigger all those old feelings. He'd told himself it was like phantom pain, a residual ache from a part of him that had been torn away.

But there was nothing ethereal about what he'd felt earlier for Tess. And while he could blow off the anonymous sort of attraction he'd felt for her during the drive from Casper yesterday, he couldn't dismiss this so easily. What kind of man got all lathered up over a nursing mother?

He stalked blindly down the aisle, so familiar with the big barn's layout that he didn't even see the row of stalls to either side or the hayloft above his head. Instead, he concentrated on carefully hanging the pitchfork on the outer wall of the tack room, rather than hurling it at the nearest object, the way he wanted to.

For some reason, the small demonstration of will helped. At least enough that he could finally face the rest of what was bothering him. As much as he wanted to deny it, something had...happened...to him last night. In the instant when he delivered the baby, he'd felt closer to Tess than to anyone ever before in his life.

An aberration, he told himself firmly. An illusion born of the moment. Not all that surprising, really. Birth was a profound experience and, hell—he was only human.

It didn't mean anything. So what if it had felt good to be needed? So what if he'd felt that startling sense of connection? So what if he'd felt a compelling urge to take care of her, to treat her like a queen, the way his dad had treated his mother, the way he himself had once treated Elise?

He'd learned his lesson. Being open and trusting and generous had brought him nothing—unless you counted the loneliness, the anger, the heartache he'd lived with the past three years.

He was never going through that again. He was never

going to care about anyone so much that he couldn't walk away unscathed.

The reminder served to steady him. He reached over and picked up a clean bucket, then flipped up the hinged lid of the grain bin and dipped it inside. At the familiar rustling sound, nine equine faces popped over the tops of their stall doors, liquid eyes expectant.

The familiarity of the horses' reaction eased him further. He stripped off his gloves and stowed them in his pocket, then started down the row, taking his time as he fed each of the four mares and five geldings a few handfuls of oats. By the time he got to the end of the line, the gentle tickle of velvety muzzles had lightened his mood even more.

Obsidian, a rangy gray Jack had raised from a foal, stamped his feet as he waited his turn. Jack shook his head but obediently held out a portion of oats, careful to keep his hand flat as the horse greedily scraped at his palm. "Take it easy, you old reprobate." He tugged on the gray's silky forelock. "Bite me, and I'll have a talk with those fine folks who make dog food."

The gray gave a snort that conveyed his opinion of that.

Too bad people weren't so easy to understand, Jack thought with a rueful sigh. Still, it was time to quit belly-aching, to put the past two days in perspective. So there was something about Tess that got to him, so what? He'd had itches he couldn't scratch before. Eventually they went away—and so would she. In the meantime, she'd no doubt divide her time between sleep and taking care of the baby; Elise hadn't gotten out of bed for a week after she gave birth. All he had to do was keep his distance, and in a day or two the weather would improve and they'd part company.

This time next month, she'd be a dim memory.

He fed Sid another handful of oats, gave him one last

pat and yanked on his gloves. He switched off the lights and shrugged back into his heavy coat, then did up the buttons, wrapped a scarf around his lower face and neck. Bracing himself, he put his shoulder against the door and slipped outside.

The wind snatched at him, tearing the door from his grasp and nearly knocking him to his knees. He staggered, only to get lucky as he blindly reached out and encountered the guideline he'd strung the previous night. Holding tight, he pulled the safety loop over his head and around one shoulder.

Normally, the trip to the house took less than a minute. Now, it took five times that, and the visibility was so poor he didn't know he'd reached the porch until his boot hit the first step and sent him sprawling.

He climbed to his feet, cursing a blue streak. He found the stair rail and clambered up the stairs and across the porch. He stopped under the shelter of the overhang. Shivering, he slipped off the safety loop and slapped the snow off his coat and jeans before he tramped into the mudroom.

He unwound the scarf, wondered briefly where the dogs were, his thoughts fuzzy from the intense cold. Deciding he'd wait to shed the rest of his outerwear in the relative warmth of the kitchen, he pushed open the inner door, only to grind to a halt at the discovery that the room was already occupied.

"What are you doing here?" he demanded of Tess, too shocked to temper his voice when he saw her standing by the stove, whisking something in a bowl. The tantalizing scent of frying bacon made his stomach cramp with hunger, while the blast of heat from the fire she'd built in the big fireplace drew him like a magnet. The dogs, the furry traitors, were already there, fast asleep.

"Fixing something to eat. I don't know about you, but I'm starved. I hope you like pancakes."

It wasn't right. She was supposed to be in bed, too wiped out to do more than sleep and concern herself with the baby.

Instead, she'd helped herself to a pair of his thick thermal socks and another of his flannel shirts, this one an oversize blue-and-black plaid, which she was wearing with a pair of stretchy blue pants that must've come from her overnight bag. She'd also showered; her thick chestnut hair had regained its high-gloss sheen and her pale skin had a warm tint of color. She looked a little tired, but it didn't detract at all from the provocative tilt to her mouth.

Goodbye perspective. Hello itch.

She poured batter onto the gas range's built-in griddle. "The coffee's fresh, if you'd like some."

He stripped off his coat and gloves, stalked over and poured himself a cup. He started to take a sip, then stopped. "Where's the baby?"

She pointed to a kitchen drawer sitting in the middle of the table. "Right there. I wasn't quite up to wrestling the cradle down here, but I read somewhere that a drawer would work as a baby bed in a pinch."

He scowled, walked over and critically inspected the makeshift crib, taking in the thick blanket she'd used for padding. The baby, thoroughly if sloppily covered, was wide awake, blinking up at the ceiling. He set his cup down and tucked the blanket more firmly around her, and she promptly switched her focus to him. Even though he told himself not to be foolish, he could have sworn her sweet little face brightened at the sight of him.

He stepped away and sent a hard look at the infant's mother. "You ought to be in bed."

"Probably." She flipped the pancakes. "But I'm not.

These won't take very much longer. Why don't you go wash up, and then we'll eat?"

He wanted to refuse. He wanted to order her upstairs and tell her in no uncertain terms to stay there. He wanted to inform her that she had no right to intrude any farther into his life than she already had.

On the other hand, he was hungry, breakfast was almost ready, and pancakes and bacon were his favorites. Why cut off his nose to spite his face? It was one damn meal, not a long-term commitment. He'd eat, he'd ignore her, and that would be the end of it. "All right." He went to wash.

By the time he got back, Tess had moved the baby to one end of the rectangular table, set a pair of places, and was already seated, a fragrant stack of steaming pancakes, a platter of bacon and a ceramic bowl filled with canned peaches in front of her.

Jack sat, as well. His movements deliberate, he filled his plate, dropped his napkin onto his lap, and began to eat, not speaking except to ask Tess to pass the syrup. He felt her scrutiny but ignored it, and after a moment she, too, began to eat. Relieved, he concentrated on taking the edge off his hunger. He polished off a dozen fair-size pancakes and a like amount of bacon slices in a matter of minutes.

Without saying a word, Tess laid down her fork, stood and strolled to the oven. Grabbing a hot pad, she retrieved a second plate of pancakes, walked back, took one for herself—it was her second—and slid the rest onto his plate.

She sat and picked up her coffee cup, waiting patiently as he methodically demolished his second helping. When he was almost done she inquired politely, "Were the horses all right?"

He nodded.

"How many do you have?"

"Nine."

She swallowed a sip of coffee. "That's all?"

He shrugged. "Spring and summer, two or three times that." He resumed eating.

"You take care of that many horses all by yourself?"

He pointed at her plate with his fork. "Your food's getting cold."

"That's all right." She looked at him expectantly.

He sighed. "I have a pair of hands who help out." Her expression didn't change, and his mouth twisted sardonically. "Brothers. They're in Mexico now. Visiting family."

"Ah." She nodded and took another sip of coffee. "So what do you do with the horses?"

"Train them."

"To do what?"

"Cut cattle."

"For whom?"

"Rodeo circuit, mostly." He ate another pancake.

Her eyes narrowed speculatively. "You mean, you train horses for professional cowboys?"

He nodded again.

"But...those horses are expensive." Since it wasn't a question, he didn't respond. "And you're here all alone... Why don't you have a cell phone? As isolated as you are, I'd think you'd want one as a hedge against emergencies."

He set down his fork. "Not everybody wants to reach out and touch someone. Some people like to be alone. Some of us—" he gave her a long, level stare "—prefer it."

She regarded him thoughtfully. "I take it that means you don't want to talk about yourself?"

"You got it."

"All right." At last there was a slight edge to her voice.

She put both hands flat on the table, pushed back and stood.
She began stacking plates.

"What do you think you're doing?"

"The dishes."

He pushed back his own chair and rose. "I'll take care
of them. Why don't you take the baby and go upstairs?
Rest or something."

Her eyes glinted dangerously. "Fine." She set down the
plates with a clunk. She took a few steps sideways, only to
stop. A trace of uncertainty showed briefly on her features.

"What's the matter?" he inquired.

"Nothing. I just—" She pursed her lips, then raised her
chin. "Would you mind taking a look at her diaper first? I
tried to copy what you did, but it didn't look right."

He shrugged. Whatever it took to get her out of there.
He came around the table, irritation prickling through him
when she moved over but didn't entirely step away.

He pushed the baby's covers aside and deftly stripped
away her too-big plastic pants. Underneath, she was clean
and dry, but it was no thanks to the diaper. It was the
sorriest mess he'd ever seen, loose and lopsided, sagging
clear to her dimpled knees. "What's this supposed to be?
Some sort of origami?"

"Very funny."

He unfastened the pins. Told himself to shut up. And
promptly heard himself say, "Haven't you ever changed a
baby?"

"Yes. Of course. But I used *modern* diapers. You may
not know it, but you can actually buy them to size these
days. With safe, reusable tapes instead of sharp, outdated
pins."

"Those disposable things?" He snorted. "They're bad
for the environment. Besides—" he shook out the long

rectangular cloth, refolded it and deftly pinned it into place "—all this takes is a little practice."

"Right." A trace of amusement crept into her voice. "So why don't you go a little faster? That way I could feel even more inadequate." With a slight shake of her head, she leaned forward and gently touched a finger to her daughter's small hand.

He could smell the faint fragrance of soap on her skin. That trapped, edgy feeling crept back, and the silence suddenly felt oppressive. He stared down at the baby. "What's her name, anyway?"

"I don't know yet."

He turned to look at her, then was sorry when his abrupt motion brushed his shoulder against hers. "You're kidding, right?"

"No. I was so sure she was going to be a boy…" A touch of asperity entered her voice. "I didn't pick a girl's name. And before you ask, I've never given a child a bath, or taken a temperature, or done any of the rest of that, either."

"Terrific," he muttered.

"But I'll learn. After all—" she looked down at the blue blanket, then back up at him, a mixture of challenge and something that looked suspiciously like compassion in her eyes "—you did."

His jaw bunched. Damn her. She saw too much.

Without saying a word, he wrapped up the baby and handed her to her mother. "Thanks for the breakfast."

Tess met his gaze over the infant's head. Eyes locked, they stared at each other, neither of them giving an inch. And then she gave an unexpected sigh. "You're welcome." With that, she turned, crossed the room and started up the back stairs.

Jack stayed where he was, watching her ascend until she

disappeared from sight. His face felt tired, the muscles stiff from the control it took not to expose his whirling emotions.

His insides felt as tangled as ever.

Four

"Here." Jack tossed the book on the kitchen counter. "I thought maybe you could use this."

Tess let the plate she was washing settle to the bottom of the sink and leaned over to take a closer look at the oversize paperback. The title jumped out at her: *As Easy as ABC: Taking Care of Baby from Birth to Age 3.*

She tried to decide whether to be amused or offended.

Amusement won. After six days, it was clear that not all parents were created equal. Her diapers still sagged, her swaddling shifted, and she had yet to settle on a name for her daughter. As for Jack...well, he might not be big on conversation, but, as the gift of the book indicated, neither was he as aloof or as indifferent as he pretended.

Not that he wasn't doing a great imitation, she thought, twisting around as the door to the mudroom banged shut behind him. That first day, after their breakfast together, he'd braved the bitter cold to return to the barn, where he'd

stayed for the rest of the day. When he had come in, it had
been well past dinnertime and he'd been in no mood to
chat. Moody and monosyllabic, he'd switched on the radio
and eaten dinner out of a can. His attitude hadn't improved
when he heard the weather forecast, either; he'd seemed to
take it as a personal insult that the storm battering Montana
and Wyoming was predicted to last through the weekend,
still two days away. Minutes later, he'd announced he was
going to bed and had withdrawn into his study, firmly shutting the door behind him.

It had been all of seven-thirty.

Since then, Tess had hardly seen him. Either he'd been
out in the barn or closeted in the study. He showed up at
mealtimes to slap together a sandwich or heat a can of chili,
but he didn't linger and he didn't indulge in any idle chit-
chat.

Clearly, he was avoiding her. And it bothered her; she
wasn't sure why. Maybe because he'd shared the most profound moment of her life. Maybe because of her certainty
that he'd suffered some sort of major heartbreak. Or maybe
because there was a desperate quality to his aloofness; despite his attempts to appear cool and callous, he kept slip-
ping up with small acts of kindness—like finding her the
book.

She glanced at the item in question and came to a sudden
decision. She wiped her hands on a towel and headed for
the utility porch. Hoping to catch Jack before he left the
house, she yanked open the door—and crashed right into
him.

"What the—!" He dropped the armful of bridles and
other tack he was holding, grabbed her as she stumbled
back, then caught her close as she swayed forward.

Tess froze, not prepared for the feel of him, big and
warm and solid against her open palms. Nor for the way

his scent filled her head, a delicious combination of soap, cold air, horses and a faint trace of spicy aftershave.

"You need something?" he demanded, setting her firmly away. His tone implied that whatever it was, it had better be good.

She raised her chin. "Yes, as a matter of fact. The baby's starting to smell a little ripe. I wondered if you'd have time later to help me bathe her?"

He was shaking his head before she finished the sentence. "Look in the book. That's what it's for."

"I'm sure it has good advice," she said patiently. "But it can't tell me where to find the things I'll need, like soap and shampoo and extra towels. And I'm not sure what I'm supposed to do about her umbilical cord—"

He gestured at the tangle of leather littering the floor. "I've got tack to clean."

"I could help."

His green eyes narrowed dangerously in the dim light. "Look," he said abruptly, "it's like I told you. I've got better things to do than take care of you and the kid. Remember?"

"Oh, I remember." She wasn't likely to forget.

Last night, after Jack had made his usual retreat to his study, she'd listened to the radio for a while and straightened the already neat kitchen. Then she'd taken the baby upstairs, fed her and put her down to sleep. She'd changed into her borrowed nightshirt, picked up the paperback mystery she'd found on a shelf in the living room, crawled into bed to read and had promptly fallen asleep.

Hours later, she'd awakened to the deep rumble of Jack's voice. Although the words had been indistinct, his inflection had been so soft and gentle, so achingly tender, she'd thought she was dreaming. When she'd surfaced enough to open her eyes, however, she'd found he really was just a few feet away, silhouetted by the light from the fireplace. Bemused, she'd realized he was talking to the baby. "Jack?"

He'd jumped as if she'd zapped him with a cattle prod. "You're awake."

"Umm. Sort of." She'd looked around for a clock before remembering there wasn't one. "What time is it, anyway?"

"A little after midnight."

She'd sat up and pushed the hair out of her eyes. A shock had gone through her when he'd turned fully toward her and she'd seen that his jeans were unsnapped and his shirt undone, providing a stunning view of a shallow navel, a washboard stomach, a lightly hairy chest hard with muscle. For some reason, she'd found it hard to swallow. "What... what are you doing here?"

For an instant he'd looked nonplussed. Then, suddenly, he'd gone on the offensive. "What do you think? I came to see what was wrong with the baby."

She'd stared at him, considered the relative silence and wondered what he knew that she didn't. "What do you mean?"

A slight tic had throbbed in his jaw, then miraculously subsided as little—Amber, Jade, Crystal?—let out a plaintive sputter. "That's what I mean. How am I supposed to get any sleep?"

As if sharing his annoyance, the baby had begun to cry in earnest. Galvanized, Tess had tossed the covers back and scrambled out of bed, too intent on comforting her daughter to be self-conscious because all she had on was his shirt. "I'm sorry. I didn't hear her—"

Jack had jerked away, hastily averting his gaze. "Forget it. Just try to be more alert in the future, will you? I've got more to do than look after the two of you." He'd stalked out of the room.

It hadn't been until this morning, when Tess had come along the lengthy upper hallway, descended the main staircase and looked down the hall at the door to the study, that she'd thought to wonder how he possibly could have heard the baby. It wasn't as if the little darling had been howling; while Tess might not be an experienced mother, she *was* a light sleeper, and she knew she couldn't have slept through that. After all, Jack had managed to wake her with a few whispers.

Bottom line, the man had lied. Whatever had brought him upstairs and into the master bedroom, it wasn't that the baby had disrupted his sleep.

"I remember what you said," she said carefully. "But she's so little. And if I give her a bath, she'll be wet, and if she's wet, she'll be slippery." She paused for effect. "What if I drop her?"

That revealing nerve in his jaw jumped to life. His eyes narrowed even more, but when she simply stared inquiringly back at him, he finally gave in. "Aw, hell. All right. Now go inside, would you? You're letting cold air into the kitchen." He stooped and began to gather up the tangle of halters, bridles and other items he'd dropped.

She wasn't about to argue. Returning to the kitchen's comforting warmth, she checked on the baby—Katy? Karen? Katrisha?—who was still fast asleep, then returned to the sink to finish up. Jack came in a minute later. He set the tack down on a chair, got an oilcloth to cover the table, gathered a stack of clean rags, a round tin of saddle soap and a bowl of warm water. In minutes, he was hard at work.

She might have been invisible for all the attention he paid her.

Tess set the last dish in the drainer and went to join him. Intent on the bridle he was dismantling, he appeared not to notice as she selected a piece of toweling, wet it, worked it across the saddle soap and picked up a cinch strap.

But then again, appearances could be deceiving. "Don't get the leather too wet," he said abruptly.

"I won't." She diplomatically didn't point out that she'd grown up cleaning tack. Not just because she had a few questions and a favor to ask, but because she also felt overdue for some adult company and she didn't want to give him an excuse to bolt.

Instead, she worked the soap into the cinch, taking her time, doing it right. Not until she was totally satisfied did she pick up a fresh piece of toweling and begin to dry it, stropping it through the towel in her hand. "Jack?" She inspected the leather.

"Humph."

"I've been wondering...how do you train cow ponies if you don't have any cattle?"

There was a moment of dead silence when she thought for sure he wasn't going to answer. Finally, however, he said coolly, "Your grandma supplies me with a few head as I need them. Right now I don't."

"Oh." It was the last explanation she'd expected. Still, it explained how he'd known Mary would be gone. It also opened up a whole new category of questions. "How is she?"

"Mary?" He shrugged. "I don't know. Why don't you ask her when you see her?"

Then again, maybe not. He was about as chatty as a grizzly bear with a mouthful of porcupine. With an inner sigh, she laid the cinch aside and reached for a headstall. She removed the bit, and pulled the throat latch, headpiece and chin strap free, letting the silence spin out before she spoke again. "Jack? Would you mind if I did some cooking? Maybe started taking care of lunch and dinner?"

His hands stilled and his head came up. "Why?"

"Well, it's not to poison you, so you don't need to sound so suspicious." She rubbed her rag across the soap. "And it's not to pay you back for all you've done, because that's a little more involved than providing a few meals. The truth is—" she glanced up and gave him a quick, wry smile "—if I have to eat another peanut butter sandwich I'm going to start sounding like Jimmy Carter."

He stared stonily at her for a few seconds longer than was polite, shrugged and went back to work. "Suit yourself. There should be some stuff in the freezer."

An understatement. She already knew the appliance in question was packed side to side and rack to rack with enough food to feed a small army for a year. Still, that didn't interest her as much as his stubborn refusal to lighten up. "Thanks."

Again, he shrugged his wide shoulders. "Thank my mother. She does the grocery shopping."

"Oh. That's nice. Does she live around here?"

"No."

"Where does she live, then?"

"Rapid City."

"Is that where you grew up?"

"No."

Be patient, Tess. "Where did you grow up?"

"Cattle ranch east of there. My mom sold out after we lost my dad."

"I'm sorry," she said, meaning it. "Is that when you bought this place?"

"No."

Oh, for heaven's sake! She snuck a peek at him, trying to decide if he was hoarding words for a purpose or just to drive her crazy. It didn't take more than a second to realize the futility of the gesture; not only didn't she have a clue what went on behind those leaf green eyes, but the longer she looked at him, the more aware she became of his intense masculinity. She found herself thinking about last night, about his muscled chest and the modeled flatness of his bare belly. An odd flutter kicked up inside her...

Good grief, where had that come from? she wondered, a little wildly. True, new moms were prone to some weird postpartum hormone imbalances. But still— She drew a shaky breath.

"Look," Jack said sharply, misconstruing the cause of her distress, "my mother sold the family ranch twelve years ago, okay? I've been here six. In between, I spent some time on the rodeo circuit."

"Really?" She latched eagerly on to the subject; anything was better than where her imagination had taken her. "I wanted to do that. When I was fifteen, my consuming ambition was to be the first woman allowed to ride broncs on the men's circuit."

"Yeah?" His gaze flicked over her. "What happened?"

"I turned sixteen and decided what I really wanted was to be a rock star like Madonna."

He couldn't hide a flash of reluctant amusement. "Oh. Well. I guess that's normal."

She widened her eyes. "Wanting to be Madonna?"

One black brow slashed up, giving his face a mocking cast. "No. Kids having idols."

"Who were yours?"

He shrugged. "I don't know. My dad, I guess. And Gaylord Perry. My brother always said—" He stopped. His hand tightened on the rein he was holding. A glob of orange saddle soap oozed up between his fingers.

Without thinking, Tess reached out to wipe it off. "Your brother always said what?"

The curve of his mouth abruptly flattened out. "Nothing.

Forget it." He looked down at her hand touching his and jerked away with such force his chair skidded a few inches across the floor. He stood. "I have to go. There's something I forgot to do out in the barn," he said tersely.

She couldn't have heard him right. "You're kidding. Now? Surely it can wait—"

"No. It can't." He gestured at the tack strewn across the table. "Leave this. I'll finish it later." Turning away, he snapped his fingers at the dogs, who were dozing in front of the fire. "Tucker. Kite. Come on. Let's go."

"But, Jack— Hey, wait." She clambered to her feet. "I don't understand—"

The dogs crowding his heels, he kept walking, leaving her to stare blankly at the door as it slammed shut behind him.

All she could think was that he was nothing at all like Gray.

She squeezed her eyes shut, shaken by a sudden wave of loneliness. *Damn you, Gray Maxwell. How could you go off and leave me like this? You were the one who was good at reading people—not.*

She sighed. Lord, but she missed the guy. Not as the lover he'd been for one single, solitary night, but as the anchor, the sounding board, the best friend and confidant that he'd been for nine years.

He'd been funny, smart and kind. And—in stark contrast to Jack—direct, open and easygoing. If he'd been a body of water, he would have been a backyard pool—warm, clear, inviting.

Jack, on the other hand, was white water, turbulent, unpredictable, quicksilver, possessed of hidden depths, stomach-dropping dips, uncharted twists and turns.

Gray had made friends wherever he went.

Jack was so very much alone.

She heard the outer door slam. She walked to one of the windows that overlooked the yard and twitched aside the curtain, narrowing her eyes against the onslaught of white outside. For the moment, the wind had fallen off, but the snow continued to come down, steady and relentless, wrapping the countryside in muffled silence.

From the right, the dogs bounded into her field of vision. They leaped wildly through the ear-high drifts, their plumed tails waving exuberantly despite the chill. Jack appeared a moment later, wading through the snow that been blown onto the path to the barn since he made his last trip.

She had only a brief glimpse of him before he rounded the corner, but it was enough. His head was down, his shoulders were hunched, his mouth was a compressed line. He looked as bleak as the landscape.

Tess sighed. She didn't understand him. She wasn't sure she wanted to. But she was beginning to believe that, more than anyone she'd ever known, Jack could use a little friendliness, a little softness, in his life.

She stared out at the vast sea of white and thought about that for a long, long time.

A promise was a promise.

A man's word was his bond.

There was a sucker born every minute.

Of the three, Jack knew damn well it the last one that best explained why he was standing in front of the kitchen sink with his shirtsleeves rolled up and his hands full of wet, slippery baby.

It didn't matter that the baby in question was a charmer. Or that she looked pretty darn cute as she cooed up at him from the warm, shallow water.

He should never have agreed to this. He should have stuck to his guns when he told Tess she could find all the help she needed in the child care book. Barring that, he should have refused to honor his commitment. God knew, everybody else did.

But not him. It was a rude shock to find that some part of him still believed in the same old outmoded code of honor. And though he had nobody to blame but himself, he knew exactly who was a contributing factor to his foolishness.

He glanced sideways at Tess, who was doing the baby washing while he did the baby holding, and cataloged her most recent sins.

First she'd cleaned the rest of the tack, willfully ignoring his assertion that he'd take care of it later.

Then she'd fixed dinner. Not just any dinner, but fried chicken, with mashed potatoes and gravy and all the fixings, and chocolate cream pie for dessert. She'd brought a tray of it to his study, left it even though he'd told her he wasn't hungry—and hadn't said a word when he showed up in the kitchen for seconds.

By the time he'd finally finished eating, she'd already done the rest of the dishes, scoured and disinfected the sink and had the child care book open to the "Giving Your Baby A Bath" section.

Through it all, she'd been friendly and pleasant, just as if he hadn't bolted from the house earlier without a word of explanation. Short of appearing like the biggest jerk since Attila the Hun, he'd had no choice but to roll up his sleeves and keep his word.

But he didn't have to like it.

Or her.

Broodingly, he gave her another surreptitious look.

Her lush, pink mouth was pursed with concentration. And she'd done something to her hair, piling it on top of her head in such a haphazard fashion that several silky strands had escaped to cling to her cheeks and temples like fine copper threads. She also seemed to be having trouble keeping her clothes on. Her shirt was partially open, with enough buttons undone to expose all of her satiny throat and enough of her full, firm breasts to make any healthy, red-blooded man squirm.

Frowning, Jack realized he was shifting his weight from foot to foot and forced himself to stand still. He transferred his gaze to the baby, who rewarded his scowl with a lop-sided lift of her mouth.

"Oh, look!" Tess exclaimed. "She's smiling at you."

"It's gas," he said flatly.

She rolled her eyes and leaned close to the baby. "It is not, is it, pumpkin?" She scooped up a handful of water and dampened her daughter's dark curls. "She likes you."

"She's not old enough to know what she likes." Lucky kid, he thought caustically, shifting his weight again as Tess scooped more water and her arm rubbed against his.

"Why do you do that?"

"Do what?"

Tess straightened and reached across him for the shampoo. "Always assume the worst."

He shrugged. "Beats the hell out of thinking like Pollyanna. At least you're prepared when things go to hell. Which they will."

Incredibly, she smiled. "Oh, I don't know. I always thought hoping for the best made good sense."

"I bet you also think the light at the end of the tunnel is a light," he said caustically, "and not the train."

"So?" She poured a scant amount of shampoo into her palm and carefully swished it through her daughter's ultra fine hair. "If it *is* the train, what good is knowing that going to do? You're just going to waste a lot of time worrying about what you can't change."

He shook his head, frustrated by her naive attitude. "Maybe you have to get run over to understand."

Her hand stilled, and she twisted around to look at him. "Maybe I have," she said evenly.

As simply as that, he found himself replaying the exchange he'd been trying to forget for a week.

I bet the kid's father is thrilled.

Save your sympathy. He's dead.

Damn, damn, damn. He stared blindly down at the sinkful of water, cursing a mental blue streak as all the questions he'd been avoiding about the man who'd been the baby's daddy crowded his throat.

Had the other man wanted his child? Had he even known about her? If he had, why the hell hadn't he married his baby's mother? How had he died? What happened to him?

The plastic cup Tess was using to rinse the baby's hair froze in midair. She swung her head around, her face mirroring a concoction of surprise and disbelief. "I'm sorry. What did you say?"

He took in her expression, then could have kicked himself as he realized he must have spoken that last out loud. "Nothing. It wasn't important. Forget it."

They stared at each other. He could see her uncertainty, and he realized with a sinking feeling that she was still trying to decide if he'd really said what she thought he had. To his relief, she didn't pursue it, however. "All right," she said finally, inclining her head. She resumed rinsing the baby's hair. "There. That should do it."

"Great." Five minutes more and he was out of here. Trying not to appear too eager, he slid one hand beneath the baby's back, took a hold of her upper arm so that she wouldn't squirm away and gently lifted her up, transferring her to a thick pad of towels on the counter.

Tess stepped close, caught up the edges of the topmost

towel and wrapped it loosely around her child. Then she grabbed another and began the drying-off process, starting at the baby's head and working her way down. "Gray had what's called a hypocephalic glioma," she said quietly, her attention all for her daughter. "A form of brain tumor. Swift onset, lightning growth." She paused to lift the baby so that she could dry the back of her neck. "Last January he began to have headaches. Some problems with his vision. By the time he saw a doctor, it was too late. He was diagnosed in February, gone six weeks later." Satisfied that all the baby's wrinkles and folds were dry, she dusted the little girl's bottom with baby powder, reached for a clean diaper and began to fold.

Jack couldn't think what to say. "I'm sorry," was what he settled on finally, the words sounding inadequate as hell, particularly after his recent remarks about Pollyanna and trains. "It must've been tough."

She frowned at the diaper, shook it out and started over. "Yes. He was one of the real good guys. Like the pumpkin here." She sent her daughter a melting smile.

He heard a soft drumming and realized he was tapping his fingers against the counter. Damning his inability to stay still, he whisked the diaper out of her hands. "Here. Give me that." He made a few swift adjustments and slid it into place.

Tess carefully wielded the pins. "Thanks."

"You're welcome." To his disgust, he sounded anything but. He capped the shampoo, then let the water out of the sink as she began wrestling the baby into a clean sleeper.

"Jack?"

"Hmm." He wrung out the towel they'd used to pad the slippery porcelain and slapped it down next to the pile on the counter.

"About what happened earlier. I'm sorry if I did something to offend you."

His whole body tensed. He didn't want to think about that, much less discuss it. "Forget it. It didn't have anything to do with you." It was the truth, he thought fiercely. It hadn't had a damn thing to do with her and the uncanny way she had of getting beneath his defenses. It had been about him, and about hopes and dreams and old times best left forgotten. "I thought I'd left a space heater on out in the barn," he lied.

"Ah."

He could see that she didn't believe him. He told himself he didn't care about that, either.

The baby started to fuss, making the impatient mewing sounds that indicated hunger. He watched as Tess fastened the last snap on the sleeper, lifted the little girl up and cuddled her against her shoulder. Just for a second, he remembered what it had been like to be touched with such sweetness.

It was a struggle to keep his voice even. "Go ahead and go upstairs. She's hungry. I'll finish cleaning up."

"But—"

"Go. I want to catch the weather report, and I can't hear anything over all that caterwauling."

A faint flush rose in her face. She opened her mouth as if to protest, then shut it. "All right. Thanks for all the help. I guess I'll see you in the morning." She went across the room and up the stairs, pausing as she reached the corner landing. "Hey, Jack?"

"What?"

"Sweet dreams," she said softly. She disappeared from view.

Sweet dreams? Oh, God. His entire body jerked as the idea wrapped around him, as soft and enticing as her voice.

He rubbed a hand over his eyes. He hadn't had a decent night's sleep since he met her.

He rolled his shoulders and tried not to think about how much a part of his life she'd become in only a week. Instead, he repeated the words that were beginning to sound like a litany: The sooner she was gone, the better.

With any luck at all, that shouldn't be much longer. According to the most recent forecast, the storm was expected to end sometime in the next seventy-two hours. Once it did, it might be another day or two before the roads were passable, but after that, he'd take Tess wherever she wanted to go and then his life would get back to normal.

All he had to do was hang on a little while longer.

Five

The sunrise began as nothing more than a shimmer of light.

Soon, however, fingers of pale yellow streaked the dawn twilight. The sky lightened, gray to lavender, pink into blue, azure to aquamarine, while the flame-red edge of the sun rose higher. A tide of gold washed slowly across the frozen landscape.

"Well, damn it all to hell, anyway," Jack muttered, staring balefully out the kitchen window. Except for the sparkling clouds of snow that danced before the gusting breeze, nothing moved across the frost-silvered terrain. Not a bird or a jackrabbit or a coyote could be seen.

Sure as shooting, it was going to be another lethally cold, treacherously windy day. A day when travel was impossible.

A day just like the previous nineteen.

Jack gave a little shudder as he recalled the pep talk he'd

given himself the night he helped Tess give the baby that very first bath.

Three more days he could have handled. Three more weeks was proving impossible.

No matter how often he told himself to dwell on the positive, to be grateful that at least the power and phones had come back on and that they had plenty of food, fuel, firewood and the other necessities, it didn't change one crucial fact: With each day that passed, he came closer and closer to losing the battle he was waging to keep himself aloof from Tess.

He heard a familiar step on the stairs. He didn't have to turn to know it was *her,* in search of a cup of coffee.

"Morning," she said softly, passing behind him.

As usual, she brought with her the now familiar fragrance of shampoo and soap on warm, moist skin and he knew she'd already showered. As usual, the smell went right to his head, filling it with visions of dim, steamy enclosures and long, lissome limbs and water-slick flesh—

No wonder he felt so edgy, so restless, so expectant. *Nothing like a self-inflicted dose of frustration to start off the day.*

He took a deep breath, listening as she took a cup from the drainer and lifted the glass pot from the coffeemaker. He heard her approach. His muscles strained in silent protest as she scooted close enough to read the thermometer attached to the siding on the other side of the glass. "Wow. Thirty below." She gave a theatrical shiver and turned to him with a sunny smile. "It's colder than it was yesterday."

"I noticed." She didn't have to sound so damn *pleased,* he thought sourly.

"How cold do you suppose it is with the windchill figured in?"

He considered a distant stand of leafless trees hunched beneath the breeze. The wind had been ceaseless the past pair of weeks, rarely falling below twenty miles per hour, and often gusting to two or three times that. "I don't know. Fifty, sixty below."

"You know, I don't remember it ever being this bad when I was a kid."

He grunted. "Maybe because it wasn't. Didn't you hear the guy on the news last night? This is the longest stretch of subzero weather Wyoming's seen since they started keeping records." It was also the first time in the six years he'd lived there that the snowplows had been too busy to get to his road. According to the county, unless he had a medical emergency, he was low-priority, since they were already stretched thin just trying to keep the main roadways open.

"Hmm," she said agreeably. She wrapped both hands around her coffee cup and took a long swallow, regarding him above the rim. Her eyes were big, dark, thoughtful. "So—" she lowered the cup and cocked an eyebrow "—is it the weather that's got you down? Or did you just roll off the wrong side of the couch this morning?"

He wasn't about to dignify that with an answer. Instead, he sent her his best black look. The one that always intimidated store clerks and gas jockeys and could be counted on to silence his mother when she started fussing at him.

Tess reached out and patted him on the shoulder. "Maybe some food would help. How about breakfast?"

Didn't she ever lose her damn composure? "No. Thanks."

She gave him an assessing look, then nodded. "All right. Then how about this." For once, she sounded a little uncertain. "I think I've decided on a name for the baby."

"Yeah?" He tried to sound uninterested and failed.

"Yeah." She took a deep breath. "How about…Nicole? Nicki, for short."

He considered a moment, then nodded, ashamed to admit, even to himself, that there was a part of him that was relieved she hadn't chosen Grace in honor of the late Gray. Not that he cared for himself, of course, or had a proprietary sort of interest; he just didn't think the baby looked like a Grace. He nodded. "Yeah. I like it."

Tess smiled. "Great."

Her eyes met his, and he felt that alarming sense of connection stir. He looked hastily away.

Tess took another sip of coffee. "What are you up to today?"

"The usual."

"Ah. See to the horses, work on the books?"

He nodded.

"Don't you ever get tired of the same old routine?" she asked mildly.

"No."

"Never?" She strolled over to the coffee pot and freshened her cup.

He glanced at her. Something about her looked different. She seemed taller, slimmer…

"Because I was thinking—" her voice deliberately casual, she turned to look at him over her shoulder "—that maybe you'd like some help this morning."

He jerked his gaze from her fanny to her face. "With what?"

"The horses."

He shook his head. "Forget it."

"But, Jack—"

"No way. You have to be here with the baby."

She made an impatient gesture with her hand. "I just fed

her and put her down. You know darn well she'll sleep for at least another hour. Maybe two.''

That much was true. Unlike her mother, the baby—Nicki-Nicole, he amended, trying it out—was the most amenable, most agreeable and least troublesome female Jack had every known. Although only three weeks and three days old, she'd already settled into a predictable schedule. "So?"

"So it's not as if she's going to crawl out of her cradle and wreck the place if I step outside for half an hour. Heck, she probably won't even roll over. She seemed really tired this morning. You'd think she'd been up half the night or something.''

She looked straight at him. He could see the speculation in her eyes, but he ignored it. If some nights he couldn't sleep and chose to walk off his restlessness in the hallways, and if sometimes the baby stirred and was lonely and he was near... Well, there was no cause for Tess's concern. She ought to be grateful that she got an extra hour or two of undisturbed sleep.

"Please, Jack? I'd really like to see the horses.''

"No.''

Frustrated, she took in his expression and seemed to realize that nothing she said was going to change his mind. Even so, she let the look between them lengthen before she finally raised her chin and said, in that controlled way that always set his teeth on edge, "Fine. Tomorrow, then.'' She turned away and walked toward the fridge, turning her back on him and any further objections. "Now. You have any requests for dinner?''

You bet. Thirty-degree weather. You to go away and leave me in peace. Some relief for the constant itch beneath my fly. He rolled his shoulders, feeling trapped in his own skin. "Whatever.''

She shrugged, but didn't turn. "Suit yourself."

"Yeah, right."

Tess listened to the door close behind him.

How often in the past two weeks had she heard that sound? Thirty or forty times? A hundred, if she added in the solid snick of the den door swinging shut?

One time too many, she thought darkly. She wheeled away from the refrigerator, slapped her cup down on the counter before she threw it at something and paced across the floor.

Darn it. Every time she thought she was making progress, connecting with Jack in some small way, she would get just so far and then *wham!* He'd slam a door, either real or mental, shutting her out, ensuring that she stayed away.

If she wasn't so happy, she'd be miserable.

The absurdity of the thought made her miss a step. But it was the realization that it was absolutely true that stopped her in her tracks. Feeling slightly light-headed, she stood smack in the middle of the kitchen and asked herself why, but the truth was she already knew.

A large part of her contentment could be attributed to the baby. She was crazy about Nicki. Like the best of all miracles, her and Gray's daughter might have been conceived during the harshest of sorrows, nurtured during a time of great uncertainty and born under circumstances that had been less than ideal, but that only seemed to make the restored sense of joy she'd brought to Tess's life all the more special. Tess felt as if the baby's birth had completed a circle, linking her with her past, providing a bridge to the future. Despite a long-term responsibility that was awesome, having a child felt right.

So did coming back to Wyoming. She'd known she missed it, but she hadn't realized how very much until her plane touched down in Casper. It had been as if a weight had lifted off her shoulders. Gone was the restlessness that had plagued her teenage years. She'd left to get an education, to see the world, to find herself. Having done that, she'd come home because she wanted to. The vast plains, the huge sky, the solitude—even the extreme weather— made her feel complete, as if some part of her that she hadn't even known she was missing had been restored.

Not that she had any illusions. While she was happy at the moment to cook and keep house, to eat, read, sleep and spend hours marveling at the absolute perfection of her daughter, she doubted it would be enough to fulfill her much longer. Already she felt plagued with excess energy. She might revel in her motherhood, and be certain her future belonged in Wyoming, but soon she was going to need something more to keep her busy.

Something like cleaning stalls and hauling hay and getting to know the Cross Creek horses.

Damn Jack, anyway.

Well, what did you expect? This is the same guy who in the brief space of days after it stopped snowing and before it started blowing spent a day and a half with his fanny frozen to a tractor seat trying to clear a path to the road so he could get rid of you. Did you really think he'd welcome you into his private domain just because you asked?

Of course not. It was almost as unrealistic as her hope that she could fundamentally change his outlook on life with a few smiles and a little friendly conversation.

A reluctant grin twisted across her mouth. Talk about being arrogant! After the break with Mary, her only family, she'd spent nine years proving she could make it on her own and telling herself she didn't really need anyone. It had taken a tragedy and a blessing—Gray's loss and her pregnancy—to make her finally see how much she needed other people and to admit that they were what mattered, not money or success, not excess pride or always being right.

Why she should expect Jack to see things the same way simply because she willed it was a question she'd been asking herself for days. She'd pondered it almost as much as she had the problem of how to make him stop seeing her as a nuisance and start to see her as a woman.

Because she could no longer deny that she had feelings for him, even if most of the time he was difficult, aloof, evasive and unfriendly. He made her feel alive.

Tess sighed. A reasonable, sensible, prudent woman would give up. But the truth was, she'd never been any of those things. On the contrary, she'd always liked a challenge.

Still, she had to admit she was getting extremely tired of having doors shut in her face. It was clearly time for a change in strategy.

The question was, to what?

The following day brought no change in the weather.

Jack narrowed his eyes against the late-afternoon sunshine cursing the cold as he slid open the big barn door and stepped outside. The wind cut right through him, despite so much clothing—two pairs of socks and two sets of long underwear, flannel-lined jeans, a wool shirt, a down vest, an insulated duster, gloves, hat and a muffler—that he felt as overstuffed as a Thanksgiving turkey. Adding to his discomfort, the fine film of sweat he'd worked up doing evening chores was already freezing to his skin, while his fingers, toes, ears and nose had begun to ache.

He tried to ignore the discomfort, fixing his attention instead on the big bay mare named Cassiopeia at the other end of the reins in his hand. Making a soft clicking sound, he led her outside, slid the door shut, then set off for the arena. The mare danced along beside him, nearly pulling his arm from the socket as she jumped nervously at every shift of shadow and rattle of wind.

He pushed open the arena door and led her inside, shaking his head when she eyed the shadowy interior as if she'd never seen it before. "Settle down now, darlin'," he murmured, his breath billowing in the frozen air. His movements slow and deliberate, he reached up, gathered the reins, planted his foot in the stirrup and began to ease himself into the saddle. He continued to talk in that same soothing undertone. "Easy, now. It's okay, there's nothing to be afraid of—"

The mare wasn't buying it. The instant she registered his weight, she gave a giant shiver and flung herself sideways, doing her damnedest to scoot out from underneath him.

Jack quickly swung the rest of the way up. He'd barely touched denim to leather, however, when the mare abruptly dropped her head, planted her front feet and let loose with a crow hop that rattled his teeth.

"Aw, for heaven's sake." He shortened the reins and sat down hard to show her there was a price to be paid for her bad manners, then gave her a sharp rap with his heels and set her at a brisk walk around the rails. At first she continued to shy at every little shadow and sound, but eventually his gentle, soothing voice and quiet confidence began to pay off. The mare relaxed, giving him her trust. A faint smile touched his mouth. After a few more circuits, he nudged her into a slow, controlled trot.

Despite his easy posture, he could feel the strain in his muscles. Normally, he spent anywhere from three to six hours a day in the saddle, depending on the number of horses he had in residence. Now, however, with the extreme cold and the demands of doing all the chores single-handed, he was lucky if he could manage an hour. That meant the horses were getting about a tenth of their normal weekly exercise. Since they were also confined to the barn, their energy level was high and their nerves were on edge. Just like his.

So? You had an offer of help and you turned it down.

He gave a snort, his mouth flattening out, at the reminder. He and Tess had gone another round about that at lunch today. God, but the woman was stubborn! She refused to accept that he meant what he said and there wasn't a thing she could say that would change his mind.

She just didn't understand that more time with her was the *last* thing he needed. Not when he already knew more about her than he wanted to.

He knew she didn't like broccoli, that she had a thing for new wave Irish folk music, that she loved to read and could juggle numbers faster in her head than he could do on paper.

He knew she'd spent the past few years in San Francisco, where she and the baby's father had owned a successful import business together. He knew she'd traveled all over the world as the company's buyer and that she'd recently sold the business and didn't have to worry about money.

He knew she had a temper. He knew it wasn't in her nature to pout, that she didn't expect to be entertained, that she didn't consider the ranch the middle of nowhere, the way Elise had.

He knew she sang in the shower, slept on her side and looked a heck of a lot better in his shirts than he did.

He knew Mary Danielson's abrupt decision to take a vacation had hurt her.

He knew the more he learned about her, the harder it was to keep a proper distance.

And he knew he spent too much time thinking about her. Like that foolishness yesterday, when he'd gotten it into his head that she looked somehow different. He'd been pondering it off and on ever since, had even caught himself staring at her like a randy teenager at the oddest moments, trying to figure out why he was so fascinated by the swell of her fanny and the curve of her hips—

He straightened in the saddle. God. That was *it*. How could he have been so blind? Why had it taken him this long to realize that for the first time since he'd met her, her shirttail hadn't been out? Instead, it had been tucked into her jeans, providing him with an unrestricted view of her very pretty backside.

Except that she didn't have any jeans. All she had were those stretchy things. Which meant... Well, hell. It meant that the damn jeans must be *his*.

Jack froze, transfixed at the thought.

Unfortunately, it was at that exact instant that one of the barn cats darted out of the shadows and dashed beneath Cassiopeia's feet. The skittish mare gave a violent start, seemed to leap straight up, then came crashing down onto a patch of frozen ground, only to have her front legs slide out from beneath her.

Jack never had a chance. One moment he was thinking about Tess and his purloined pants. In the next he was sailing over the mare's head and hitting the ground with a force that made him see stars. A second later, Cassiopeia fell on top of him.

For a while after that, he didn't see much of anything.

Tess settled deeper into the oversize chair by the kitchen fireplace. Trying not to smile, she gazed with exaggerated curiosity at her daughter, who was cradled in the crook of her arm. "Okay, kid. What's your secret? Why do the same dimpled thighs that look so bad on Mama look good on you? Come on, now—give.''

The baby stared intently at her, big blue eyes wide in her little face.

''Not talking, huh?'' It was amazing, Tess thought. After only three weeks and a few days, she couldn't imagine her life without Nicki in it. She felt enthralled, tender, protective and besotted, as saturated with love as a soggy sponge. ''I guess you're just naturally diplomatic,'' she told the baby, leaning down to kiss the silk-soft little hand clutching her fingers. ''Either that or you've been taking lessons in stonewalling from your buddy Jack.''

The baby frowned. For a whimsical moment, Tess thought maybe it was an editorial response to her comment about a certain cowboy, and then, with the sort of psychic communication she still marveled at, she understood. She eased the child up and rubbed her back, smiling when Nicki gave a very unladylike belch. ''My sentiments exactly.''

At least one of them had a full tummy, she thought, her smile fading as she glanced at the clock. Dinner was ready, but she'd held off, waiting for Jack, who should have come in forty-five minutes ago.

She wondered uneasily if something had happened to him. Then she told herself not to borrow trouble. It was far more likely that he was simply taking his time, in no rush to come in after the exchange they'd had earlier in the day. The one in which she'd reiterated her desire to help and he'd said he'd consider it when hell froze over. To which she'd responded that it seemed pretty darned cold to her all of a sudden, prompting him to get his fanny in a sling and stomp off to the den, where he'd stayed until time to do chores.

Tess sighed and shifted the baby into a more comfortable position. ''Losing my temper wasn't exactly part of my new strategy for winning him over,'' she confided to her daughter. ''But then, I don't have your advantage. I'm not small and sweet and adorable. I can't make him melt just by looking at him. As a matter of fact, I think it's safe to say that mostly I annoy him—''

She broke off, saved from further confidences by the dogs. Like a shaggy warning system, they suddenly surged to their feet, trotted to the door and began to whine in anticipation. A few seconds later, the door swung open and Jack came in.

Tess took one look at him and felt as if a giant fist had squeezed her heart. His hair was disheveled, his coat, jeans and boots were dirt-stained and snow-caked, his face was chalky, his mouth strained. He had his right arm pressed protectively against his side, his gait was unsteady, and he was shivering.

She scrambled to her feet and hastily laid the baby in her makeshift bed. ''My word! What happened to you?'' She hurried toward him.

His jaw tight, he swung the door shut with a careful flick of his left wrist. ''Nothing.''

''Right.'' She snapped her fingers at the dogs, who were dancing around him, and pointed at the fireplace, using the seconds while they made their reluctant retreat to get herself under control. ''You always come in looking like this.'' She made a broad gesture that enveloped him from neck to toes.

He looked down, surprise flickering across his face as he took in the state of his clothing. He sighed. ''Okay. So I had a little problem.'' He headed unsteadily in the general direction of the sink, stopping before the cupboard where the medicine was kept.

Tess followed along in his wake, not certain what she felt most at that moment, concern or exasperation. ''Like what? A horse fall on top of you?'' He glanced sharply at her, and with a pang of dismay she realized that her facetious comment had been dead on target. ''Good Lord,'' she murmured.

He ignored her. He opened the cabinet and took out the aspirin, moving with obvious difficulty. He stood there a minute, contemplated it, and then, with an exasperated sigh, turned and held it out to her, his expression stony. ''Open that, would you?''

She took the bottle, twisted off the cap and poured a trio of tablets into his waiting palm, then grabbed a glass from the drainer and filled it with water. She took a deep breath and tried to match his detachment. ''So...is the horse all right?''

''Never better.''

''And what about you? Do you think anything is broken?''

He grimaced. ''No. Just bruised.'' He tossed back the tablets and took the glass, spilling a little of the water when his hand shook.

He needed heat, she thought. Inside and out. ''Can you make it over to the chair by the fireplace?''

He narrowed his eyes, the ultimate tough guy. ''Yeah.''

''Then why don't you go sit by the fire, and I'll bring you a cup of coffee?''

He started to shrug, then thought better of it. She watched as he made his way painfully across the room. Willful as ever, he passed the chair she'd mentioned and stopped instead in front of the fireplace, where he stood, head bent, soaking up the heat.

Tess dragged her gaze away from his broad back, unnerved by the contradictory emotions racing through her. Part of her felt fiercely protective and wanted nothing more than to walk over, smooth back his rumpled hair and somehow ease his pain. Part of her wanted to bury her head against his shoulder and sob with relief that he was all right. And part of her wanted to clobber him for daring to get hurt in the first place.

Shaking her head, she made a quick trip to the utility room. By the time she approached him with the coffee she'd promised, she had herself firmly under control. "Jack?"

He opened his eyes and took the cup she held out. He took a long swallow. She noted with relief that his hand was steady; the heat from the fire seemed to be doing its job.

He lowered the cup. "Thanks." He took another gulp and set it on the mantel.

"No problem." She reached up and began to unsnap his coat.

He gave an involuntary start, sucked in his breath at the pain from the imprudent action, but still had the strength to grab her by the wrist, stilling her movement. "What do you think you're doing?"

"Getting you out of these clothes so we can get a look at the damage."

He released her and took a step back. "Forget it."

She took a step forward. "Not a chance."

"I'm warning you, Tess—"

"What?" Her actions deliberate, she reached out and calmly undid another snap. "You're going to stop me?"

"That's right."

A faint shiver racked him. She raised her gaze to his and decided it was time to quit pretending. "Listen to me, Jack," she said, her voice trembling a little as she thought about what a close call he'd had. "As cold as it is, you could have died out there. If you're right and you've only got some bruises and a mild case of hypothermia, then that's great. But let's at least make sure."

"Fine. I can manage myself—"

"I'm sure you can. But after everything you've done for me, stopping after the accident, delivering Nicki…" She paused, never taking her eyes from his. "I'd like to help. Can't we declare a truce?"

He stared at her, his gaze searching her face before he abruptly looked away. "Aw, hell." He reached for the cup and tossed back half the contents as if it were straight whiskey instead of mere coffee. "All right. If it'll make you feel better…"

"It will." Before he could change his mind, she quickly undid the rest of the snaps on the khaki-colored duster, unzipped the quilted green vest underneath and unbuttoned his black wool shirt. Next, she undid his cuffs and tugged his shirttail out of his jeans, trying not to let herself think too much about the intimacy of what she was doing as she reached up and slid her hands between his shirt and his navy long-john top. "Left side first, okay?"

He nodded and set the mug back on the mantel, so that he could help as she pushed all three layers of clothing off first his left shoulder and then his right. "Leave them," he ordered, when she leaned forward to pick them up off the floor and brushed against him.

"All right." She straightened, trying not to stare when she saw how the knit top clung to the solid muscle in his arms and chest. She took a shallow breath. "This next part is going to be a little tricky."

"Just do what you have to," he said curtly.

"All right." She took a firm grasp on his left cuff and helped him free his arm from the close-fitting fabric, then carefully began to inch the shirt up his left side, one palm skating up his arm while the other worked the fabric up his chest. The first time he quivered when she brushed her fingertips against his rib cage, she thought she'd imagined it. But when it happened again, her fingers stilled and she glanced up in concern. "Am I hurting you?"

"No."

She didn't believe him. There was the harshness of his tone for one thing. For another, the nerve in his jaw was ticking like a metronome. She moved even more carefully. Biting her bottom lip in concentration, she slid her warm fingers over his cool skin with agonizing slowness.

"For God's sake! Would you hurry up and get it over with?"

The explosive sound of his voice startled her so badly she found herself clutching the velvety bulge of his biceps. She whipped up her head. "Yes! If you'll quit yelling at me!"

They stared at each other, practically nose to nose. For the space of one endless second, Tess found herself wondering when the room had gotten so unbearably hot. And why she suddenly couldn't remember how to breathe. And why she couldn't seem to look away from the brilliant green of Jack's eyes, except to gaze at his mouth, which seemed unbearably, undeniably, excruciatingly beautiful...

And then she couldn't think at all. She could only echo the low groan that exploded from deep in his throat and thrill to the solid feel of him as his good arm encircled her and he tugged her close. To her shock, every nerve ending in her body suddenly throbbed with desire. It seemed the most natural thing in the world to part her lips as his head dipped down. And to sigh with pleasure when his mouth closed over hers.

His lips were cool and firm, his body was hard and enticing, the kiss was hot and hungry. It was everything she'd anticipated, in every way—except for the sweetness. That

was devastating and unexpected, hinting at a vulnerability
she'd begun to think existed only in her imagination. She
was as unprepared for it as she was for her response to it:
a sweeping need that stole the last of her breath and made
her blood race.

Shamelessly she twined her arms around his neck and
pressed closer, fiercely glad for the first time in her life for
the height that made it possible for her to come up on her
toes and rock her pelvis against his.

He groaned. Louder than the first time. His body strained
against hers, and he opened his mouth, deepening the kiss.
Incredibly, it was hotter, sweeter, even better...until the
persistent rasp of a buzzer intruded.

Like a man awakening from a dream, Jack went still,
stiffened, then slowly raised his head, ignoring her vague
murmur of protest.

She pressed a kiss to the underside of his jaw, then to
the pulse in his neck, unable to think of anything appropriate to say. Awash as she was in a languorous haze, it
took her a while to realize that the shoulder beneath her
cheek was rigid with tension. She lifted her head. And felt
the first stirring of uneasiness when she saw the cool, shut-
tered look on his face.

Instinctively she tried to head off whatever it was he was
going to say. "Jack. Wait—"

"That," he said flatly, stepping away, "was a mistake."
With a controlled savagery that froze her in place, he
reached up and jerked the knit shirt over his head, down
his right shoulder and arm and flung it to the floor.

"Oh!" She let out a soft gasp, but she couldn't have
said what distressed her more: Her first horrified glimpse
of the angry bruises already purpling his right shoulder and
side. The mortifying discovery that her milk had let down

and soaked the front of her shirt. Or his swift, unexpected rejection.

Surely she'd heard him wrong.... "What did you say?"

"You heard me. This never should have happened. I'm sorry."

He was *sorry?* She felt the blood leave her face.

The buzzer sounded again.

"What the hell is that, anyway?" Jack demanded, gazing irritably toward the utility room.

"The dryer." Under the circumstances, she couldn't decide what was more surreal, his question or her answer. "I put a shirt in to warm for you." With a further sense of shock, she realized that she'd done it no more than ten minutes ago.

It felt like hours.

"Thanks," Jack said. "But I don't need it."

"You don't seem to need anything," she murmured before she could stop herself.

She realized then that she had to get out of there. Out of the room, away from him. She had to leave before her unruly hormones combined with her wounded heart and she did something incredibly stupid.

Like burst into tears. Or smack Jack right in his beautiful, blockheaded face.

"I'd better get Nicki to bed." Blindly she stepped over to the table where the drawer-cum-baby bed sat. True to her easy-going nature, Nicki was already fast asleep. Without a word, Tess gathered the child into her arms, crossed the kitchen and went upstairs.

She was all the way to her room when her stomach growled and she realized she'd never eaten dinner.

It was simply one more thing for which Jack had to answer.

Six

Jack couldn't get his vest on.

Frustrated, he stood in the middle of the kitchen floor and tried to convince himself that this was just a minor setback. Okay. So he was running a little late this morning. And yes, the horses should have been fed an hour ago. But given how bad he felt—stiff, sore, exhausted and out of sorts—he was doing his best. Just as soon as he got the damn vest wrestled into place, he'd be out the door.

He gathered himself for another try. First he hunched his aching right shoulder to keep the quilted material from sliding off, the way it had twice before. Then he reached up, pulled the vest across his back, released the fabric and quickly attempted to push his good arm through the armhole.

To his relief, he finally seemed to have it. He slid his fingertips down, found the opening on his first try, and had just started to slide his hand through when a cool, feminine voice sounded behind him, catching him by surprise.

"Morning," Tess said quietly.

Startled, he twisted around. It proved to be a bad mistake. Pain exploded along his right side. His stomach rolled, and he swayed, struck by a wave of pain-induced vertigo. Perspiration popped up across his nose and prickled between his shoulder blades. Muttering a stream of invective, he cursed the weakness that left him shaking and jerked his hand free of the vest to reach across his chest and clutch his throbbing shoulder.

Seemingly oblivious of his predicament, Tess came the rest of the way down the stairs and strolled past him on her way to the coffeepot. A faint frown marred her face when she saw that it was empty, a situation she quickly set out to remedy. She put a filter in the basket, filled it with fresh grounds from the canister on the counter, picked up the glass carafe and carried it over to the sink. "I thought you'd be gone by now," she said after she filled the vessel with water, as if only then remembering he was there.

He narrowed his eyes. Despite her casual tone, there was an edge to her voice that he'd never heard before. "Well, I'm not."

"What happened? Oversleep?"

"Something like that." He wasn't about to admit that he'd actually spent a miserable night huddled in the chair by the fireplace, unwilling to lie down for fear he wouldn't be able to get back up again. It didn't concern her, any more than his secret suspicion that the only reason he was as dressed as he was because he'd been unable to get his boots off last night.

Bottom line, it was none of her business if he felt lower than pond scum. Not when she seemed so fresh and energetic, with her skin all flushed from her shower and her hair as shiny as his mother's mahogany sideboard. Not when she was so sublimely unaware of him, while every traitorous inch of his body ached at the mere sight of her. And particularly not when he'd made a mistake the size of Texas by kissing her last night.

Even if she had seemed to enjoy it...

She walked past him again, and her soft, clean fragrance filled his head. Carefully he turned to keep her in view as she moseyed across the room, stepped lightly over his discarded long-john top and opened the screen on the fireplace. She stirred the coals and added a log to the fire. "Aren't you worried that the horses must be getting hungry?"

To hell with the vest. "I was just on my way out." He limped over and grabbed his coat, which earlier he'd tossed over one of the kitchen chairs.

"Ah."

There was something in that "Ah" that stopped him in his tracks. "What's that supposed to mean?"

To her credit, she didn't pretend not to understand. Still, she thought a moment before she answered. "I suppose it means you'd better leave me your mother's phone number."

"Why," he asked, trying not to lose his temper as she walked back toward the kitchen for coffee, forcing him to turn yet again, "would I want to do that?"

She took a mug from the cupboard. "Because when somebody dies, it's customary to notify their next of kin."

"Well, thanks for the concern, but the last time I checked, tardiness wasn't classified as a capital offense."

"No, but you won't last five minutes out in the cold dressed like that."

"Like what?"

She made a distinct sound of exasperation. "Oh, for

heaven's sake, Jack. Get a clue. You not only don't have your long underwear on, but your shirt's not even buttoned.''

He looked down, saw she was right and managed a one-shouldered shrug. "I just haven't gotten to it."

"Of course not. You were too busy celebrating your iron-man status doing handsprings."

"Yeah?" he said rashly. "Well, I wouldn't be in this condition if you'd keep your own damn clothes on."

"What on earth does that mean?"

Good God. Why couldn't he keep his mouth shut around her? "Nothing," he muttered, struggling to get his coat on. "Forget it."

"No. I want—"

"This isn't about what you want," he said, interrupting her. "Hell, it's not even about what *I* want. You grew up on a ranch. You must know that, like it or not, the stock has to be fed." Unable to do any better with his coat than he had with his vest, he gave up in disgust. He stuck his good arm in the sleeve and simply draped the other side over his sore shoulder. He took an unsteady step toward the door.

"Then let me do it."

"What?" He stopped and turned to stare at her, sure he must have misunderstood.

Tess didn't blame him. She could hardly believe she'd made the offer herself. Not after last night. After last night, he didn't deserve more than a quick shove out the door, unless it was a kick in the tush to go with it.

Except…he was hurting. Enough that it was a struggle for him to put on his coat. And no matter how much she told herself he was a stubborn, insensitive, unfeeling oaf—and that *she* was nine kinds of fool—it bothered her to see him in pain. Even if he deserved it.

Besides, she could use the fresh air. She squared her shoulders. "I said I'll do it."

"Yeah, well…thanks for the offer, but…no. It won't work. You don't know where anything is, or who gets what, or who bites and who kicks—"

She resisted the urge to point out that if he had let her help out before, the way she'd wanted to, none of that would be a problem. Instead, she said reasonably, "You can tell me."

He looked skeptical. "I don't think so. There's too much to remember—"

"I had a baby, Jack, not a lobotomy. I can write it down."

"And there's an awful lot of heavy lifting," he went on, as if she hadn't spoken. "It's only been what—four weeks?—since you had Nicki…"

"It's closer to five. And I'm a fast healer."

"If something happened—"

"Nothing's going to happen. But if something did, you'd take care of it, just the way you've taken care of me and the baby and everything else these past few weeks." To her chagrin, her absolute conviction rang in her voice.

Judging from his sudden silence, Jack heard it, too. Separated from him by no more than a half-dozen feet, Tess could see the expression in his eyes change—from impatience to surprise to something that closely resembled dismay.

But surely that wasn't right. Why would he dislike the idea that she felt he could be depended on?

"You're not going to let this go, are you?" he said abruptly.

She studied his tired face and decided that now was not the time to pursue it. She shook her head no.

He sighed. "All right, then. If you're sure…"

"Yes. I'll get a pen and some paper." She did just that. Moments later, they sat down at the kitchen table together.

Warily at first, and then with increasing ease, they went over the barn's layout, identified each horse's stall, discussed the various animals' personalities and feed requirements, and the location of the hay, grain, vitamins and other supplements. Jack also explained how to check the heating unit on the tank that automatically supplied water to each stall.

Half an hour later, armed with several pages of instructions, Tess was finally ready to go. She glanced over at Jack. He was sitting back in his chair, his weight resting carefully on his left side, his long legs, in their dusty jeans, stretched out in front of him.

She wondered idly how he'd managed to pull on his boots when he couldn't manage something as simple as his coat—and felt her heart contract as the answer came to her. She suddenly understood why he had on the same clothes he'd worn yesterday. And why he had yet to shower, when the hot water would feel so good on his stiff muscles...

She came to a sudden decision. Quickly, before she lost her nerve, she stood, came around her chair and knelt at his feet.

He tensed. "What do you think you're doing?"

"Your boots are dirty," she said, careful to avoid his gaze. "And I washed this floor just yesterday." She knew him well enough by now to know he'd resist any suggestion that he couldn't take care of himself, and under the circumstances it was the best she could do.

She grabbed hold of a boot and tugged. It took a considerable amount of muscle, but eventually it slipped off. She set it aside, then repeated the procedure with the other one.

"Tess..."

She looked up. A mistake, she realized, as she found herself caught by the incredible green of his eyes. The specter of last night's kiss suddenly hovered between them. She could practically feel his mouth on hers, hot and drugging. And recall how cool and soft his hair had felt against her fingers. And remember the excitement that had twisted through her as she'd pressed against him and felt the warm weight of his sex thrusting back.

Her breath caught, growing hot and heavy in her throat as his eyes grew heavy-lidded. She came up on her knees. Let her eyes drift closed—

"You'd better get going," Jack said roughly.

Her eyes flew open. She was just in time to see him jerk back in the chair. "Of course." She surged to her feet, her face hot with mortification. What the heck was wrong with her? Why couldn't she seem to stop throwing herself at him? She was all the way across the room and had her hand on the doorknob when he finally spoke.

"Tess?"

She stopped, but didn't turn. "What?"

There was a long pause before he said quietly, "Just... take care of yourself out there."

Jack was asleep when Tess got back.

He was sprawled in a chair in her bedroom. Typical of Jack, he'd moved the chair so that he could keep an eye out for her, positioning it between the baby's cradle and the window that looked out on the barn.

A single glance told her he'd showered. His dark hair was fresh-washed-glossy, he had a pair of nicks in his chin from what she had no doubt had been a stubborn try at left-handed shaving, and he'd changed into a clean white shirt and an ancient pair of faded button-fly jeans.

Nicki, who was also asleep, was on his lap, her bottom

propped on a pillow and the rest of her securely cradled in the crook of his left arm.

Tess couldn't take her eyes off the pair.

She stood as still as a statue a few feet away. She could feel the chilly wash of air from the unheated hall at her back. She knew she ought to turn around, retrace her steps and close the door.

She didn't. And though she told herself she was merely reluctant to do something that might disturb their slumber, on some level she suspected that the weakness in her knees might also have something to do with the decision. Besides, it wasn't often that she got to observe Jack without him observing her back. Why deny herself such a simple pleasure?

So she stayed where she was and indulged herself. She noted that his inky hair had grown so much since she first met him that it now touched the bottom of his collar. That he had a slight bruise on his right temple from yesterday's accident. And that even in sleep, the hold he had on Nicki was unwavering.

But then, he didn't look much more relaxed asleep than he did when he was awake. His strong features were still dark, dangerous and moody, and the line of his mouth was taut. The only soft thing in his face was the short, dense brush of inky eyelashes against the hard curve of his cheek.

It was an unsettling discovery. It had been her experience that most people looked gentler, kinder, or at least more benign in repose.

But not Jack. And the worst of it was, it didn't matter.

Maybe it was her recent exposure to so much fresh air after so long inside, but at some point in the past few hours she'd come to grips with some hard truths. One was that what she felt for Jack was more than mere gratitude. Another was that while she still wanted to be his friend, she also wanted to be something more. Something special.

Because she cared about him. So much so that maybe—just maybe—she…loved him.

A rueful smile tugged at her mouth. Okay. There. She'd said it. She wasn't certain yet, much less ready to declare herself. She was simply acknowledging the possibility. Even though she supposed that meant she had to concede that her melting response to his kiss had been prompted by something other than postpartum psychosis…darn it.

Her smile faded. She could joke, but the truth was that whatever she eventually decided, Jack wasn't going to make anything easy. While it was obvious he desired her physically—God bless the conspicuous nature of male anatomy—she was under no illusions that he'd welcome her feelings. But then, that seemed to be pretty much par for the course for Jack. He seemed determined to deny himself even the most innocent pleasures, from something as basic as owning a TV to spending time with friends and family to admitting to his own good, decent nature. Heck, even kissing seemed to be on his forbidden list, as he'd made quite clear last night.

She sighed. It was ironic that the same event that had jolted her into facing her feelings had simply given him another excuse to avoid her.

Jack opened his eyes. "You're back."

"Yes." She stared at him in surprise. For a few seconds there, she would have sworn he actually looked happy to see her.

"I guess I dozed off for a second."

"I guess so."

He frowned and sat up straighter. Careful not to disturb the baby, he scrubbed a hand across his face, grimacing as the movement jarred his shoulder, but doing it anyway. "Everything go all right?"

Her heart melted a little as his hand dropped away and she saw the concern in his eyes. "Sure. It went fine. The horses were hungry, but they were all well-behaved except for the gray, and I fed him first, just the way you told me."

"What about the mare? Were you able to get a look at her?"

She walked over and sat on the edge of the bed. "She's a little stiff and has a slight bump on her near front knee, but otherwise she checked out okay. I'd say she came out of the encounter better than you did."

He grunted. "Anything else?"

She shook her head. "I don't think so. Everything was exactly where you said, the horses are beautiful, and the exercise felt good. Except for the cold, I enjoyed myself."

There was a moment's silence. Jack looked around the room. "This place looks different."

She hadn't done that much. She'd removed the frilly curtains and left the more functional shades in place. She'd replaced the fussy bedspread with an old wedding-ring quilt she'd found in the linen closet, taken down the canopy and yanked the checked slipcovers off the chairs, exposing the original blue corduroy. The room was now a little shabby, but infinitely more homey—which he knew perfectly well, given his sporadic late-night visits. "I asked you about it, remember?"

"I wasn't complaining. It looks better."

"I'm glad you feel that way." Encouraged, she gathered her courage and her thoughts. "Jack?"

"What?"

"About last night—"

The familiar guarded expression slammed into place on his face like a drawbridge coming down. All semblance of camaraderie vanished in an instant. "There's nothing to discuss."

"Actually, there is." She linked her fingers together in her lap, took a calming breath and told herself she could do this. That she had nothing to lose and everything to gain. "I've been thinking about what happened." That was certainly true. "I've decided you were right."

There was a moment's dead silence. "About what?"

She stared fixedly down at her hands. "About us getting involved…sexually. Obviously, it wouldn't work."

"Well…yeah. Obviously."

She glanced up and found he was staring at her with his eyes narrowed intently. She smiled, doing her darnedest to appear relieved. "Oh, good," she said blandly. "I was afraid you wouldn't understand."

There was another beat of silence. "Understand what?"

"The way I responded. The way I practically plastered myself to you. It's just…" She trailed off, searching for exactly the right words. "The truth is, it's been a long time since I've been kissed. And, what with that, and all the hormone changes these past few months— Well, I realize now it wasn't you. It was just…the moment. Just…one of those things."

For the space of a heartbeat, you could have heard a pin drop. "Oh."

"Not," she said hastily, not wanting him to think she was trying to hurt his feelings, "that it wasn't pleasant. It was. It was really quite—" she searched for exactly the right word "—nice."

He stared at her with a look she couldn't decipher. He nodded. "Nice."

She let out a gusty sigh. "But of course you already knew all this."

"Oh, yeah."

"I just don't want things to be awkward between us, Jack." She stood up, closed the few feet between them and held out her hand. "Friends?"

His expression perfectly blank, he reached out and gingerly grasped her proffered fingers. "Sure."

A jolt went through her at the contact; from the way the nerve in his jaw quivered like a downed electrical wire, she knew he felt it, too.

Not that he let on. "I should get going," he muttered.

"Hold still a minute first." She let go of his hand, but she didn't step away. Instead, she moved closer, leaning over to examine the mark she'd noticed earlier on his forehead.

"What the hell are you doing?" he demanded, his body going rigid.

She pretended not to notice that they were so close she could feel his warm breath tickle the sensitive valley between her breasts. "This looks painful." Gently, she brushed back a thick strand of his hair to get a better look, then touched a finger as light as a feather to the nickel-sized bruise. "You haven't been having headaches, have you?"

"Not until now."

She looked down. He was staring up at her, his green eyes as dark and unfathomable as a forest pool. The seconds played out. Then, as if acting against his will, he slid his gaze from her eyes toward her mouth. A dull flush tinged his cheekbones, and his breathing increased.

It was Nicki who saved him. The baby, who'd been as silent as a clam ever since Tess first came in, abruptly emitted a squeaky wake-up call.

As if awakening from a trance, Jack wrenched his gaze from Tess's mouth with such speed he was lucky he didn't suffer whiplash. He surged to his feet. Scooting awkwardly sideways in a move that had to hurt his thigh and shoulder, he held out the child. "Here. She's awake. You'd better take her."

Short of letting Nicki drop to the floor, there was nothing Tess could do. She reached out. By the time she had the infant settled securely in her arms, Jack was gone.

She looked down at her daughter. "Great timing," she told her offspring.

Oblivious of adult concerns, Nicki's answer was to coo in excitement at the sight of her mother. Tess shook her head, but found it impossible to be out of sorts when confronted with the baby's bright little face. Besides, it was probably best that Jack had left. Another few seconds, and Nicki wouldn't have been the only female on his lap, a development that would no doubt have undermined Tess's entire "just friends" pitch.

She sat down in the chair Jack had vacated. A faint sigh parted her lips when she found it was still warm from his body. She thought about the look on his face when she'd told him his kiss had been...nice.

A smile tugged at her mouth. "You know, Nicki, I'm not positive, but somehow I don't think he liked that."

Tess could have sworn the baby chortled.

Jack, no doubt, would have sworn it was gas.

"Are you done?"

Jack tensed as Tess reached around him to retrieve his dinner plate. Her clean scent curled around him, almost as distracting as the soft weight of her breast, which she was unwittingly pressing against his arm. He shifted sideways, away from that provocative warmth, and looked up at her. "I told you I'd do the dishes."

"I know," she said serenely. "I just thought I'd clear some of these things away before I feed Nicki." Leaving him his coffee mug, she piled his silverware on the plate and whisked it away.

Jack watched moodily as she strolled toward the sink, stopping along the way to switch on the radio. When Trisha Yearwood's voice poured out in a soft but upbeat song, Tess promptly began to hum along.

She looked…good. Not that she hadn't looked good before, but now… Well, two days of fresh air and exercise certainly hadn't done her any harm. She looked healthy and vibrant and a hell of a lot more fit than anyone who'd had a baby so recently should, he thought gloomily.

Not that he cared, of course. After all, they were friends, with nothing more between them than a single "nice" kiss.

Jack scowled, hating to admit how much that particular four-letter word rankled. He found it almost as distasteful as his growing awareness that even though he still believed kissing Tess had been a terrible mistake, he wanted to do it again. And that he wanted to do certain…other things— not one of which could remotely be considered "nice."

He continued to stare at Tess. Blissfully unconcerned with his brooding, she set the plate on the counter, splashed some soap in the sink and turned on the water. Her tall, slim body swaying slightly to the music, she peered out into the dark beyond the window and gave a theatrical shiver. Then she turned off the water and headed back toward the table. She picked Nicki up out of her bed and carried her over to one of the chairs by the fireplace. She laid the baby down to check her diaper and glanced at Jack. "Did I tell you I've decided not to go back to San Francisco?"

"No."

"Well, I have."

Jack tried to tell himself her plans didn't interest him, but it didn't work. "What do you have in mind instead?"

She shrugged. "I won't decide for sure until I see how things go with Gram, but I've been thinking I wouldn't mind owning a dude ranch."

"You're kidding."

"No."

"I hear Montana is nice."

She laughed, soft and amused, as though he'd made a joke. The sound echoed through him, setting off a vague sense of yearning for...something. "Thanks for the suggestion," she said wryly, "but I think I'd prefer to be a little closer."

"Closer to *what?*"

"Home."

Words deserted him. While he'd known all along she'd eventually spend some time with Mary, he'd naturally assumed her stay would be temporary. It had never, ever occurred to him that she might decide to stick around and settle in the area permanently.

He tried to imagine what it would be like to know she and Nicki were close by. He had his answer as he was struck with an overwhelming sense of alarm and dismay. And though he tried to tell himself his reaction was triggered by the thought of her becoming part of a community that had viewed his dirty laundry and found him wanting, deep down he knew that wasn't it entirely. Deep down, it was more the idea of her being near but beyond his reach that really bothered him—and he didn't like the discovery. "Don't you think that's a pretty irresponsible thing to do to your daughter?"

Apparently satisfied that the baby didn't need to be changed, she lifted her up and sat down herself, crossing one long, slim leg over the other. Despite the receiving blanket she had draped over her shoulder, Jack had a clear view of the growing valley of pale gold skin between her breasts as she unbuttoned her shirt in anticipation of nursing the baby.

She stared at him in puzzlement. "What do you mean?"

He jerked his gaze from her breasts and climbed to his feet. "I mean," he said deliberately as he walked to the sink, "that the way of life here, the isolation and the lack of amenities, isn't for everyone. You must know that, since you hated it enough to leave the way you did." He pulled out the garbage can and began to scrape the plates.

"I never hated it," she protested. "But I was nineteen years old, and it was all I'd ever known. I wanted to go to college, try city life, see some of the world before I settled down. Only Gram wouldn't hear of it. With her, it was all or nothing, stay or go. There was no middle road. I'll never do that to Nicki."

He could hear her sincerity. He could also hear the regret in her voice when she talked about Mary. He told himself to ignore it. All right. So there was more to her leaving and staying away than he'd realized. That still didn't mean she'd be happy here now. "I still think you'd be making a mistake," he said stubbornly. "Think about all the stuff you'd be giving up. Shopping malls. Movies, restaurants, dry cleaners. Fast food. Convenience stores. A nightlife. Six months and you'll be miserable." He picked up the washcloth and started sliding silverware and dishes into the warm water.

"You aren't."

He shook his head. "That's different."

"Why?"

Exasperated, he turned around to pin her with his gaze. "Because I don't need to be constantly entertained. To have endless diversions. To have other people around telling me who and what I am."

"Neither do I."

He snorted. "You will. It's just a matter of time."

"Ah." Her gaze sharpened on his face. "Is that what happened with your wife?"

Jack shut his mouth with an audible snap. He stared at her, appalled to realize how much he'd just revealed—and by the discovery that, appalled or not, he was tempted to go on, to finally tell his side of the story and share every sordid, humiliating, hurtful detail.

Except...to what end? It was over and done. He'd vowed never again to open himself up or to need anyone. And if he did, the last person he'd want to confide all the ugly particulars to was Tess. He could just imagine what she'd think.

He hardened his expression. "That's none of your business." To underscore his point, he deliberately turned his back on her and started in on the dishes.

"Jack?"

He heard a rustle of sound. To his disbelief, he realized she was approaching. Quickly he turned on the water and made a show of rinsing a plate. Maybe if he ignored her, she'd go away. He dumped the dish in the drainer and picked up another.

"Jack, I'm sorry."

He stiffened as she walked up beside him and laid her hand on his shoulder. What the hell was wrong with her? Didn't she realize he was done with this subject?

Obviously not. "I didn't mean to pry," she went on, just as if he weren't scowling for all he was worth. "And although it's sweet of you to worry about me..."

She thought he was *worried* about her?

"...I'm not your ex-wife. You keep forgetting that I lived here for twice as long as I've lived anywhere else. My moving back isn't a whim. It's a decision that's been a long time coming." As if that settled that, she plucked a clean dish towel out of a drawer and took a plate out of the drainer.

Jack couldn't believe it. "What do you think you're doing?"

She raised her eyebrows. "I'm drying a dish. What does it look like?"

"What about Nicki? Don't you need to finish with her or something?"

"She doesn't seem to be hungry."

Lucky baby, he thought grimly. Disgruntled, he turned to confront her, to make it clear once and for all that he didn't need her help—and knew immediately that he'd made a big mistake.

She was too close. She'd been close before, of course, but somehow he'd always managed to block the memory of their one and only nice and friendly kiss from his mind.

Not tonight. He looked down into her big, dark eyes and all he could do was remember. How perfectly she fit against him. How soft and sweet and hot her mouth was. How delicious her full, round breasts felt against his chest. How her tight little fanny was exactly the right size to fill his hands.

He took a deep breath.

There was only one thing to do. He had to get out of there. Now. Before he did something really stupid. "You sure you don't mind doing dishes?"

She smiled and shook her head.

"Good." He grabbed a handful of dirty silverware and thrust it at her. "Because there's some book work I really need to go do." He braced for her protest.

It didn't come. Instead, she gave him a long, shrewd, disconcerting look and, after what seemed like a very long handful of seconds, nodded. "Well, then, you'd better go on.'' She reached out and gently relieved him of his fistful of knives, forks and spoons. "I'll finish this.''

Less than two minutes later, a little awed at how easy it had been, Jack found himself alone at his desk in the den, with the door shut and a ledger open, exactly the way he'd wanted.

So why the hell didn't he feel better about it?

Tess wasn't sure what woke her.

One moment she was dreaming; in the next she was wide awake, aware that something in the room was amiss.

Her first thought was of Nicki. She shifted her head on the pillow and peered through the darkness at the baby's cradle. Thankfully, it was drenched in a thin wedge of moonlight that made it possible for Tess to see that everything appeared fine, a conclusion that was reinforced when she heard her daughter make one of the little smacking noises that often punctuated her sleep. There was nothing distressed about the sound; on the contrary, it was perfectly normal.

Yet Tess didn't shift or move. She continued to lie there and listen, convinced she'd heard *something* out of the ordinary.

Sure enough, less than half a minute later, a shadow detached itself from the doorway and Jack padded silently into the room.

Tess forgot to breathe. Riveted, she watched as he stopped by the cradle. He sent a surreptitious glance her way, then leaned down. It took her a moment to understand what he was doing as he appeared to sweep his hand from the bottom of the cradle up, and then she realized he was pulling Nicki's covers up.

Once he had the baby tucked in to his satisfaction, he

straightened and padded back toward the door, as sound-lessly as he'd come.

Tess waited until he was almost at the threshold. After the way he'd maneuvered her into doing the dishes tonight, there was a perverse part of her that felt it was only fair he should believe he was getting cleanly away before he found out otherwise.

When his shadow reached the door, she spoke. "Jack?" she said clearly, sitting up. "Did you need something?"

He whipped around.

There was a loaded silence. She held her breath, curious as to how he was going to explain himself this time.

She didn't have to wait long to find out.

"No," he said gruffly. "I just came to tell you…you don't need to worry about feeding the horses tomorrow. I'll do it."

"Oh. That's all?"

"That's right."

"Well…sweet dreams, then."

"Yeah…right."

She smiled into the darkness, lay back down and listened as he disappeared down the hall.

When push came to shove, he really wasn't a very good liar.

Seven

Tess slept in the next morning.

Judging by the angle of the sunlight streaming in the windows, it had to be after ten, she realized as opened her eyes and pushed back the covers.

Yawning, she watched the dust motes dance in the rising currents of warmth, and tried to get up the energy to crawl out of bed and make a trip to the bathroom.

Eventually, she made it. Deciding she was on a roll when she returned to the bedroom and found Nicki still sleeping, she went ahead and showered.

The warm water helped clear her head. It did nothing, however, to improve her wardrobe, a sad fact she acknowledged as she tried to decide what to wear. Her choices were limited. She had three pairs of too-big panties, a bra that was too small, three pairs of maternity leggings, one tunic top and her long green sweater. Augmenting this delectable collection were Jack's things: three flannel shirts, his old jeans, and a pair of long underwear. While she'd never considered herself a clotheshorse, she had to admit she was starting to long for something pretty—that fit—to wear for a change.

Still, there was no use dwelling on it, she decided as she pulled on the jeans and her own green sweater. Not when she had more important things to consider, such as Jack's visit to her room last night. Every time she thought about it, a curious combination of amusement and tenderness curled through her. He tried so hard to be tough and gruff and indifferent, and yet the caring side of his nature just kept surfacing, no matter how much he tried to suppress it.

As she headed downstairs, she tried to decide what kind of spin he was most likely to put on their latest encounter. Would he apologize? Enlarge on his explanation? Or pretend it hadn't happened?

It didn't take her long to find out. One quick glance from the top of the stairs told her the kitchen was empty, while a second, longer look revealed that there was a note propped against the empty coffeepot.

She walked slowly the rest of the way down and across the room. Jack's handwriting was big and bold, and his message was direct and to the point:

Did chores. It's warmer. Have gone to plow the driveway. Back later—Jack

Tess pursed her lips and walked thoughtfully over to the window to look out at the temperature gauge. It read a balmy fifteen above.

Well, of course. Bathing suit weather. Perfect for plowing roads. She only hoped he'd remembered to take his shades and some sunblock.

She shook her head and tried to convince herself it was

no use getting angry. She'd known he was stubborn. She'd simply underestimated the extent of it. After all, while she was hardly a beauty queen, she wasn't so repulsive that men normally risked hypothermia just to avoid her.

But then, Jack wasn't like anyone else. He was stubborn and infuriating, yes. But beneath that thorny exterior there was an overdeveloped sense of responsibility, an old-fashioned kind of honor, and a truly generous heart. She knew he was worth an effort.

Even so, she hoped he froze his buns off.

The day seemed to drag on forever. She made lunch and ate it. She read. She did laundry. She nursed, changed and held the baby, who, as if sensing her tension, hardly napped. She read some more. She made popcorn on the stove, which she burned. She ate it anyway. She paced. She put a pot roast in for dinner.

She told herself she wasn't worried.

Not when the dogs showed up alone at two, cold and hungry and grateful for a place by the fire.

Not when the clock crept past three and the sun began to descend toward the far horizon.

And not when it was nearly four and Jack still hadn't shown up, not even to feed the horses.

By 4:10, when Nicki finally nodded off into an exhausted sleep, Tess made a decision. If nothing else, she could go out and feed the horses.

Anything was better than waiting. Or so told herself as she turned the heat down on the roast, ordered the dogs to keep watch over the baby, bundled up and headed out.

By the time she finished in the barn forty-five minutes later, she wasn't so sure. It might be warmer than it had been for weeks, but it was still chilly, there was still no sign of Jack, and she was thoroughly out of sorts. Before, she'd been worried, and a little annoyed. Now, she was worried, more than a little annoyed, and half-frozen. Where the devil was Jack? Had something happened to him?

She switched off the stable lights and walked outside. She was so deep in thought as she tried to decide whether she ought to go look for him that she'd taken several steps before the low rumble of sound issuing from across the yard started to penetrate. Finally, however, she looked up.

She saw the tail end of the tractor disappear into the shed. Relief swept through her. It increased, making her knees weak, when Jack appeared a minute later and slid the big metal door shut. He started toward the barn. Unaware of her presence, he made no effort to camouflage his exhaustion. It showed in the bowed set of his shoulders and in each slow, limping step.

Tess knew she ought to feel sympathetic, and she did— for all of ten seconds. But now that she knew he was all right, what she felt mostly was...anger. It surged through her, hot and potent.

She pushed away from the barn and began to walk stiffly in the direction of the house.

Jack came to a halt when he caught sight of her. "Tess. What are you doing out here?"

She stopped and glared at him. "I fed the horses."

"Yeah? Well, you shouldn't have. I would've taken care of it."

"It was getting late."

"Yeah." He frowned, regarding her with a slightly quizzical air, as if he'd finally sensed that something was wrong but couldn't imagine what it was. "I had a little problem."

"Like what?"

"No big deal. I put the tractor in the ditch and it took me a while to winch it out."

"Ah." He could have been killed. She shivered, the involuntary movement prompted by a mixture of relief that he was okay and ire at his self-imposed danger.

Jack apparently thought she was cold. "You'd better go on to the house."

"What about you?"

"I'll be in in a while. I want to check on the horses."

Well, of course. After all, she couldn't be trusted to toss a few flakes of hay into a manger. "Fine," she said tightly. Aware of his puzzled gaze, she started jerkily along the path to the house, her lips pursed and her eyes straight ahead.

Apparently he finally got it. Or so Tess surmised as she swept past and heard him make an exasperated sound, midway between a grunt and a snort. Her temper already on red alert, she swiveled around to tell him she wasn't amused—and was just in time to see him look pointedly up at heaven and give an exaggerated shrug as he started to stomp away.

Tess abruptly had had enough. Throwing caution to the winds, she gave in to temptation. She reached down, grabbed a handful of snow, molded it into a ball and took aim at his big broad back. She wound up and let it fly.

The throw went high. With a distinct *whomp*, it smacked him in the back of his head and sent his Stetson tumbling off.

He stopped where he was. He didn't move for a second, as if he couldn't quite believe what had happened. Then he reached down, retrieved the hat and carefully knocked it against his thigh to get the snow off. Finally, he turned.

Tess was ready. She let loose with another. This one caught him square in the forehead, exploded on impact and showered him from the eyebrows down with snow.

He glowered and carefully wiped it away, clearly fighting to hold on to his temper. "Why the hell did you do that?"

She shrugged. "Because you deserved it."

"Because I *deserved* it?"

"That's right."

"For *what?*"

"Oh, get a clue, why don't you? You've been gone all day! I was worried, damn it!"

"Tess—"

"You're a royal pain in the backside, Sheridan, and I probably need to have my head examined, but I care about you—fool that I am! And not as your damn friend, either!" She swooped down, scooped up another handful of snow and drew back her arm.

He drew himself to his full height and sent her a warning glance. "Don't."

She gave an unladylike snort. "Oh, please. What are you going to do? Give me the silent treatment? Hide out in the barn? Run away on your nice little tractor?" She threw the snowball.

"Okay! That's it!" He ducked and lunged at her.

She gave a shriek and dived out his way, twisting around just in time to see him sail past her, clutching the space of empty air where she'd been. Off balance, he slipped and pitched forward, crashing facedown on the snow-covered ground.

He gave a muffled groan, tried to rise, then fell back without another sound. He didn't move.

Tess kept her distance and regarded him suspiciously. "Forget it, cowboy. I'm not falling for the old dead-duck routine," she informed him. "You might as well get up."

He didn't say a word. Or twitch so much as a single muscle.

She stared at him through narrowed eyes. "Come on, Jack. It's got to be cold down there. Get up."

Nothing. She sighed. She knew she was being suckered.

Except…what if she wasn't? What if he'd cracked a rib the other day and he'd now managed to break it, piercing a lung? What if he'd knocked himself senseless on a buried rock?

What if you just admit that, sucker or not, you can't stand worrying about him another second?

She swallowed a sigh. Warily, she took a step closer, then another and another, until she was no more than a foot away from him. "Jack?" She gingerly nudged his hip with the toe of her boot. To her consternation, he groaned. For the first time, she really began to worry. "Hey…Jack. Are you all right?" She hunkered down. Swaying a little to maintain her balance, she reached out and touched her gloved fingers to his cheek.

Swift as a striking panther, his hand locked around her wrist. She gave a yelp of surprise, but it didn't do a thing to help her as he rolled onto his back. She tumbled across him, hollering incoherently with a combination of relief, surprise and outrage. "Let…me…go!"

He ignored her, his green eyes gleaming like a tiger's as he stared at her from no more than a few inches away. "You like snow?" He let loose of her wrist long enough to grab her by the front of her coat. Taking no notice of her struggles, he held her in place with one hand while he reached around and shoveled a handful of the white stuff down the back of her collar.

Tess gave a howl and tried to jerk away, only to find herself in an even worse situation when he rolled again, this time pinning her beneath him. "What's the matter? Can't take what you dish out?"

She refused to dignify that with an answer. Instead, she tried to push him off, but it was like trying to dislodge a boulder. So she walloped him on his good shoulder, for all the good it did her. Decked out in his heavy outer gear, he was better padded than a king-size mattress. "Oh, for heaven's sake," she murmured in disgust. "Get off me, you lunkhead. It's cold down here, and you're crushing me!"

He came up on his elbows, making it easier for her to breathe, but otherwise he didn't move. "You started it."

The juvenile answer made her eyes widen. As did the discovery that, despite the cold, there was a sizeable, singularly male part of him that was pressing boldly against her belly, generating enough heat to toast an army. "Jack?" she said uncertainly.

"Did you mean that stuff you said about not wanting to be my friend?"

His voice was raspy, and she suddenly saw the glitter in his eyes and the strain across his cheekbones in a whole new light. "Yes."

He squeezed his eyes shut for the barest moment. "You know this is still a mistake," he said hoarsely as he opened them.

"That's a matter of opinion."

"Tess—"

"Oh, for heaven's sake. Just shut up and kiss me, would you?"

With a hungry groan, he did just that, fusing his mouth to hers in a rush of heat.

Only this time, Tess was ready. She was ready for the sudden drop in her stomach, the needy ache that bloomed low in her belly, the haze of desire that fogged her brain. She tangled her hands in his dark, silky hair and dragged him closer. With a sensual talent she hadn't known she possessed, she parted her lips and slowly ran the tip of her tongue along the seam of his lips.

He groaned again, worked his gloved fingers under her head and met her tongue with his. Tess, who'd never been much of a devotee of French-kissing, felt almost faint with desire at the invasion of his smooth, slick warmth.

She couldn't get enough.

She shifted, wrapped her legs around his and pressed against him, aching to feel his strength and power and warmth without the bulky barrier of their clothes. And all the while, she feasted on his mouth, savored his flavor, shared his breath, trying to tell him without words how she felt.

Her heated response set Jack on fire, but it wasn't enough. He wanted to touch her. He wanted to strip her naked and cup her breasts in his hands. He wanted to yank down her jeans and thrust himself deep inside her.

And he wanted to see her face as he did it. Intent on doing just that, he rolled onto his back, too far gone in a haze of sexual need to care about snow or cold or any stiff muscles but one. He pushed her up and looked at her, his heart hammering as he took in her flushed cheeks, her swollen lips, the slumberous desire darkening her eyes.

Teetering on the edge of control, he yanked off his gloves and reached up to tangle one hand in her soft chestnut hair, while he slipped the other under her coat in search of a bare patch of skin.

He was frustrated on both accounts. While one hand struggled with what seemed like an endless amount of cotton knit and voluminous flannel, the other encountered an icy coating of snow.

Somewhere, deep down, a little voice of reason began to make a dreadful racket. *Hey, Jack. Get your brains out of your pants and pay attention. She has snow in her hair, and it's pretty damn cold out here.*

The realization pricked at him, and the little voice grew louder.

What do you think you're doing? You really want to have

sex...here? Now? Like this? Even though it means freezing off some pretty essential body parts?

Yes. Hell, yes.

Well, hell, that's noble. And what about Tess? What if you hurt her? She just had a baby, remember? And speaking of babies, what about birth control? Yours is in the house, remember? Or don't you care? Are you so desperate that nothing else matters?

Yes.

No.

No? Jack groaned, but he knew damn well he was defeated, done in by an unfortunate conscience and a sense of responsibility that didn't seem to know they were outdated—despite a recent history where they'd made him a first-class chump.

And even so, he couldn't help it. Slowly, he removed his hand from Tess's coat, squeezed his eyes shut and uttered a curse that would have made his mother faint dead away if she heard it.

It made Tess stiffen. "Jack?"

Her voice whispered over him. "Tess...we've got to stop."

"What?" Her voice was thick and soft with need—and a tinge of indignation.

"We need to go inside."

"Okay." She leaned down and nipped at his lower lip. "In a little while."

He considered letting her persuade him. It wouldn't be hard. She wanted him. He wanted her. Did all the other stuff really matter?

Yes. Damn it.

He cursed again and turned his head away from temptation. "No. Now." He framed her cold face in his hands and gently pushed her away. "Listen to me. We're both going to have frostbite if we don't get inside."

She jerked away from him, reason slowly returning to her eyes. A shiver suddenly went through her, as if she were only then realizing how cold she was.

"Come on." He urged her to sit up.

"All right." She took a deep breath, then released it as she struggled to her feet, her movements suddenly clumsy from the cold.

He stood, as well, picked up his gloves and pulled them on. He started to brush the worst of the snow from his pants and coat, only to let it go when he glanced over and found Tess standing perfectly still, watching him.

There was a brief, awkward moment as they regarded each other. He took a deep breath and braced for a scene. After all... First he'd attacked her. Next he'd ravished her. And then he'd rejected her—for the second time in three days.

To his shock, an uncertain smile slowly curved her mouth. She took a step toward him, and then hesitantly reached out and clasped his hand. "Come on," she said softly.

Jack stared at their gloved fingers twined together.

His stomach twisted as he realized that things had changed between them in the past twenty minutes. That, like it or not, there was no going back.

And that, worst of all, he no longer knew if that was good or bad.

With her usual impeccable timing, Nicki politely waited for the adults to get inside and peel off their snow-covered clothes before she woke up. Once actually awake, however, the baby began to fuss.

It was almost as if she knew the adults needed a buffer between them, Tess thought as she picked her daughter up. "Shh...sweetie," she murmured reassuringly. "Mama's here. It's okay.'' She jiggled the infant against her shoulder and watched as Jack added another log to the fire. Drawn by the promise of immediate heat, she walked over and turned her long-johns-and-flannel clad backside to the flames, sighing as their warmth washed over her.

Jack closed the screen and stood. ''Cold?''

She glanced over at him. His face was in profile to her, the austere lines of cheek, chin and nose achingly beautiful in the flickering light. ''Yes. I know it sounds strange, but I really didn't feel it…before. Not until we came inside.''

He nodded.

There was an awkward silence. He looked tired, she realized—and strung so tight he'd snap at the slightest touch. ''Why don't you go take a shower?'' she suggested.

His expression was impossible to read. ''You sure you don't want to go first?''

''Yes.'' She regarded him over the top of the baby's head, smiling faintly when the infant gave an unconvincing whimper. ''Nicki seems to be hungry, and for once she doesn't seem inclined to wait. You go ahead.''

''All right.''

Tess watched him walk away. If truth be told, she was ready for some time alone. She needed to think, to try to sort through the events of the past few hours. She'd never known she could feel the way she had outside. She'd been so swept away by desire, so wild with the need to have Jack inside her, that nothing else had mattered.

It was a stunning admission for someone who'd always prided herself on the strength of her will. Yet it was also a testament to her instinctive belief in Jack's character. She trusted him. And today, as usual, her faith had been well-founded. Despite all his tough talk—and his obvious, very impressive need—he'd put her safety and well-being first.

Although she hadn't a doubt he'd deny it vigorously.

She started to sigh, only to wince instead as Nicki's attempt to suck on her neck reminded her that she, too, had certain responsibilities. Her face softened as she glanced down at the baby, who was doing her best to look pathetic. "I'm sorry, little one. Here you've been so good, and Mama just ignores you. Come on." She sat down in the chair by the fireplace, adjusted her clothes and guided the baby into place. "Let's fill up that poor empty tummy."

Nicki's response was to grip a fistful of flannel in her little fist and latch on like a pint-size vacuum cleaner.

Tess shook her head. No wonder she felt slightly... unhinged. Between Nicole and Jack, her emotions seemed to be constantly maxed out. Yet she wouldn't change one thing that had happened—not in the past hour or week or month—for all the world's riches. She felt more challenged, more fulfilled, more *alive* than she'd ever imagined she could.

She reached down and gently smoothed a flyaway lock of Nicki's hair. Tenderness curled through her as the baby abruptly quit suckling and sent her a quizzical look. Tess could no more stop the indulgent smile that curved across her face than she could stop the jolt that went through her as she glanced over and saw Jack standing in the doorway, watching her.

She took in his damp hair, his shadowed jaw, the green glint of his hooded eyes, and her pulse skipped a beat. Barefoot, dressed in jeans that were zipped but not snapped and a faded denim shirt, he looked big and forceful and enigmatic. And yet, there was something in his eyes, in the set of his mouth...

Longing, she realized, her heart turning over.

She wondered if he knew it. Or if he'd acknowledge it if he did. Somehow she doubted it.

But that didn't mean *she* couldn't. She widened her

smile, leaving no doubt about how glad she was to see him. "Hi," she said softly.

Maybe it was her imagination, but some of his wariness seemed to evaporate. He motioned with his chin in the direction of the oven. "Something smells good."

"Pot roast. We can eat after I shower—if that's all right?"

"Sure." He came a few paces closer and gestured at the baby. "Is she about done?"

"Yes." Feeling a tad self-conscious, which under the circumstances was really ridiculous, she pulled her shirt into place and stood. "Would you mind taking her?"

He didn't move. "You sure?"

"Of course." She handed him the baby, watching as he gingerly tucked the infant against his shoulder. "I'll be back in a little while."

"Right." Jack nodded, careful to keep his expression dispassionate, afraid she'd see how much her easy manner—and that soft smile—meant to him. Already feeling off kilter, he watched her start toward the stairs, and was totally unprepared when she abruptly stopped and retraced her steps. "What's the matter?" he said gruffly, assuming she'd had a change of heart and had decided not to leave him with the baby. "You forget something?"

"Uh-huh. This." To his stupefaction, she went up on tiptoe and kissed him, joining her mouth to his in an ardent union that was all the more devastating for the fact that she didn't touch him anywhere else. Her lips were slick, warm, soft and delicious. By the time she was finished with him, he was as hard as a fence post. Without saying a word, she turned and walked away.

He stared after her, his eyes riveted by the sway of her hips, his mind reeling from the promise he could still taste on his lips. Instinctively he cuddled the baby closer and patted her on the back in the universal gesture of comfort, although he wasn't sure whose he was after—hers or his own. He did know he'd had about all he could take. Every time he started to think he understood how Tess's mind worked, she did something that left him feeling as off balance as a drunkard during an earthquake.

He was thinking about that when Nicki let loose with an enormous burp. Surprised, he leaned back so that he could see her. "Hey, what was that?"

The baby gazed steadily back, her dainty little brows raised in an expression startling like her mother's.

Jack shook his head. "Well, hell. Who knows what either of you are going to do next?"

The baby's answer was to burp again.

Jack frowned. "Listen, kid. You think you've got it rough?" He tugged at the front of his jeans. "Thanks to your mama, I can barely walk."

Still, he couldn't just stand around, he thought, filled with a sudden surge of restless energy. He might as well set the table. After a short detour to switch on the radio, he walked gingerly over to the table. Taking a firm grip on Nicki, he reached for the place mats stacked in the center, only to falter when he heard what the radio announcer was saying.

"....a long-awaited warming trend. Overnight winds will be out of the north at ten to twenty, but are expected to subside by morning. Tomorrow's daytime highs should be in the mid-twenties at Gillette, with temperatures five to ten degrees lower at Sheridan and Rapid City. The projected five-day forecast is for highs to climb into the thirties, with overnight lows at or above zero. County officials say they expect the last local roads to be cleared and open for travel by Thursday. These include Stilson, MacDwyer and Black

Gulch, as well as Johnson County Number 9 and 13. In other news..."

Jack couldn't believe it. Finally, the weather was going to improve. In another day or two, his road and all the others would be cleared and open for travel. It was the news he'd been hoping and praying for all these weeks.

So why wasn't he relieved?

Relieved, hell. Why wasn't he breaking out the Scotch to celebrate? This meant he could get rid of his unwanted guests and get back to his real life. He wouldn't have to put up with anybody asking inappropriate questions or stealing his clothes or invading his space. He'd be alone. The way he liked it. With no ties, no commitments, no pain or disappointments to bring him down.

Yet, for some reason, the prospect of being alone again didn't seem nearly as appealing as it should have. As it *had* as recently as this morning, when he was so anxious to send Tess on her way that he'd been willing to spend the whole damn day plowing the driveway to achieve it.

Why this sudden reluctance? God knew, it wasn't as if he'd miss her...much. Sure, he liked homemade meals. And he supposed it was nice to have someone around again with whom he could discuss business. And she wasn't hard to look at...

But none of that was enough, either separately or together, to cause this sudden churning in his gut. Not when his entire focus for weeks had been on effecting her imminent departure.

Unless... He considered the heavy ache in his groin. Well, hell, of course. That must be it. The answer wasn't that he didn't want Tess to leave. He did. He just didn't want her to go until *after* he'd had her in his bed.

And why not? After everything he'd gone through the past few weeks, didn't he deserve some satisfaction? Damn right he did. For once in his life, he was going to take what he wanted, and to hell with the consequences.

Nicki made a soft little sound. Jack started to glance down, then found himself looking away, reluctant to meet her gaze. With a surge of impatience, he realized his damn conscience was acting up again.

Only this time it was way out of line.

Because Tess wanted him as much he wanted her. Oh, he'd bet the ranch she probably thought of it in some sort of off-the-wall romantic way, with him cast as the black hero into whose life she was going to bring some sweetness and light. But even so, given their last two kisses—definitely not nice, thank God—she wanted him.

Who was he to disagree?

"Jack?" Tess's low voice yanked him out his reverie.

He spun around to find her partway down the stairs.

She looked...beautiful. He wasn't quite sure what it was—the haphazard way she had her hair swept up or the extra button on her shirt that she'd left undone or the way her mouth softened when she looked at him.

After more than a month of avoiding the truth—looking the other way, turning his back, leaving the room if she was in it—he couldn't deny she took his breath away.

Tess cocked her head. "Is something the matter?"

"No. I was just listening to the weather report."

"Oh." She came the rest of the way down and crossed the room, not stopping until she was so close her scent filled his head. She leaned forward to examine the baby, then raised her head, her eyes filled with indulgent tenderness as her gaze met his. "She's asleep."

"What?" He glanced down in surprise. Sure enough, Nicki's eyes were closed and her mouth was open in a slack little O.

"Poor little tyke." As light as a feather, Tess touched a

finger to a silky strand of the baby's hair. "She was up most of the day, and I guess it's finally caught up with her. Why don't you give her to me and I'll take her up to bed." She laid her hand against his shoulder.

He felt her touch as if it were a brand. Need twisted through him, sharp and strong. "I'll do it."

"Are you sure? I mean, it's no problem for me...."

Her voice trailed off as he looked straight at her, making no effort to mask the desire riding him.

A faint flush crept into her cheeks. "Jack?"

He wanted to touch her...all over. And he wanted to hear her say his name in that same breathless tone...over and over. He cleared his throat. "Earlier. That kiss. Did you mean what I think you did?"

She didn't pretend not to understand. She searched his face, and whatever she saw there seemed to bolster her courage. "Yes."

"You realize...I'm not making any promises? I was married once, and I don't intend to do it again. I don't want you to think—"

She reached out and touched her hand to his cheek. "Jack. It's okay."

"Good." He tried to sound calm. It was hard to pull off, with his heart suddenly slamming against his ribs like a pile driver. "I won't be long." He started for the stairs.

"Jack?" Her voice whispered over him, siren-soft.

He froze. "What?"

"Hurry back."

Eight

Tess sat on the couch, her legs curled beneath her, and stared into the fire. Low and steady, the flames licked at the log, curling around it with fingers of yellow, tangerine and gold.

She heard the muted thud of Jack's bare feet on the stairs, but she didn't turn. Instead, she continued to watch the fire, waiting, savoring the way her pulse picked up as his step came closer and closer.

"Tired?"

His low, raspy voice brought her chin up. She shook her head in response to his question and absorbed details: the taut line of his mouth, the strand of dark hair falling over his forehead, the way he stood on the balls of his feet as if he were ready for…anything. "No. I got to sleep in this morning. What about you? You must be beat after being out in the cold all day."

He nodded, his gaze as intent on her as hers was on him.

"A little. But there'll be time to sleep…later." He held out his hand. "Come here," he said softly.

Anticipation hammered through her, making her light-headed. She took a deep breath, waited for the moment to pass and came to her feet.

He took a step forward and framed her face in his hands. His green eyes dark with desire, he bent his head and fit his mouth to hers. The kiss was achingly gentle to start, his lips rubbing against hers in an unhurried caress that quickly had her aching for more. As if he sensed her need, his hands slid into her hair. Anchoring her in place, he angled his head, and she opened her mouth for the thrust of his tongue.

A hollow warmth swirled through her stomach. It made her knees feel watery, so she twined her arms around his neck and leaned against him, needing to feel his solid strength against her breasts and hips. She rocked her hips and he groaned, nipped at her lower lip, then ran his mouth along her jaw to the sensitive spot where it met her neck.

He nuzzled her there, out of breath. "Tess?"

"Hmm?" She pressed a kiss to his hair, enjoying the silky coolness against her face.

"I want you. But I want this to be good for you, too. Are you sure, so soon after the baby…?"

"I'm fine, Jack. Really."

"The books all say six weeks…"

"People heal at different rates. Trust me. I really am okay."

He raised his head. "All right."

She took in the raw need that made the strong lines of his face appear stark. Tenderness curled through her, and she reached up to brush a lock of hair off his forehead. "I brought the quilt from the den. I thought we could lay it here by the fire."

He nodded. He pushed the chairs to one side while she spread the heavy, flannel-backed blanket, soft side up, over the thick green rug. Unselfconscious as only a man could be, he reached into his back pocket and tossed a pair of round foil packets onto the quilt. Then he undid the buttons on his shirt, shrugged it off and tossed it over the back of the couch. Moments later, his jeans came off, along with his briefs.

Tess stared at him in awe, taking in the strong curve of his jaw, the long lean line of thigh and torso, the bunched power of his shoulders, chest and arms. His skin looked like bronze in the flickering light from the fireplace, the warm color a stark contrast to the dark hair that curled at his armpits and bisected the washboard hardness of his belly, ending in a cloud at the top of his thighs. There, just like everywhere else, he was utterly male—every taut, thick inch of him.

"Your turn," he said softly.

Her head jerked up. She could feel a wash of heat rise in her cheeks as she undid one button, then another, with unsteady fingers. She hesitated.

His expression went very still. "What? Change your mind already?"

"No." She took a deep breath. "If you have to know, I was thinking about my less-than-flat after-the-baby tummy."

Instantly, his expression changed. He stepped close. Before she realized his intent, he slipped the rivet free of her jeans, pulled her shirttail free and slid his fingers underneath the flannel. One hand slipped around her side to fill the hollow of her back, while the other slid under her waistband and settled below her navel, cradling the gentle rise of her belly. "You're perfect," he said softly, staring into her face. "Understand?"

She sucked in a breath as his fingertips brushed against her woman's mound. "Yes."

"Good." He brought his hands up and around and slid them over her breasts, and it was his turn to catch his breath. "What happened to your bra?"

"I left it off after my shower."

He cupped her soft, firm weight against his palms. His hands felt hot and hard. He lowered his head, rasped his tongue across one jutting peak, then took her nipple into his mouth and sucked, fabric and all.

Tess felt as if she were going to explode. "Jack. Oh. *Oh!*" She arched her back, the warmth in her belly exploding in a pleasure so intense it bordered on pain. She stroked her hands over his back, feeling the smooth, satiny stretch of skin over muscle. There was something terribly erotic about being fully dressed while he was naked, and it was never more true than when the warm, velvety weight of his sex nudged against her belly. Wild from the need he was creating as he suckled and stroked her, she reached down and measured the thick length of him with her hand.

His head came up in a hurry. "Don't." He closed his hand around hers and moved it away. "I'm already more than ready."

"That makes two of us," she said with a shaky breath.

"Then let's get you out of those clothes." Suiting action to words, he undid the last few buttons on her shirt and stripped it off. He stood back, his face growing taut as he looked at her full, rose-tipped breasts. He reached out and touched the end of his index finger to one stiff, swollen tip.

She shivered.

So did he. "Take off your jeans." His voice was hoarse.

The rasp of her zipper was loud in the sudden silence. Trying not to be too self-conscious, Tess hooked her fingers in the denim and worked it over her hips and down her thighs to her knees, then let it drop to the floor. She stepped out of the encircling fabric and straightened, her heart pounding with a apprehension, excitement, and shyness.

Jack groaned. "No panties, either?" His gaze traced the long slim length of her legs. He seemed to be having trouble breathing.

She shook her head and he swore, soft and sibilantly. "Thank God I didn't know that before...."

He reached out, pulled her close, and they sank to the quilt, facing each other. His skin felt hot and his fingers seemed to burn right through her as he rolled onto his back and pulled her astride his thighs. He hooked his hand around her neck and guided her mouth to his. Their tongues tangled, and Tess whimpered at the heat building between her thighs, where the rigid length of his sex rubbed against her. She made a sound low in her throat and rocked against him as he began to touch her...everywhere.

Her hands slid into his hair. She felt wild, hot, out of control.

So did he. Or so it seemed as his hands stroked over her bottom and he pulled her closer at the same time he tipped her onto her back.

He rose above her. "Are you ready?" His voice licked against her like a rasp of velvet.

"Yes."

There was a momentary pause, a tearing of foil, and then he was poised above her. He reached down to guide himself, and she felt the first incredible pressure as his shoulders rose and his hips fell, and then he was slowly, slowly sliding inside her.

He felt huge. She caught her breath and angled her hips as he pressed forward. "Oh."

Jack froze. "Am I hurting you?"

"No. Oh, no." She'd been prepared for discomfort. Instead, she felt a hot jab of pure pleasure that made her shiver. She stroked her hands down his sides and clutched at his back. "More."

He shuddered, unable to hold back any longer. He began to thrust, carefully at first, and then, at Tess's urging, faster and faster.

Breathing hard, he leaned down and fused his mouth to hers.

The pleasure started for her first. It was a hot, building pressure that grew more and more concentrated with each stroke of his body in hers. She arched, straining for more. "Oh, Jack, yes, more—"

"Tess, damn it, don't move like that—"

She felt his back hollow out, and then the pulsing warmth as his climax ripped through him and he practically lifted her off the floor. He seemed to swell inside her, and suddenly all the sensation in the world seemed to be concentrated in one sensitive, swollen spot. She pressed against him and he rotated his hips, and her world exploded in a shock wave of pleasure.

"Yes. Oh, Jack. Don't stop Don't...stop..." She wrapped her arms around him and held on.

Together, they rode out the storm.

It was after ten when they finally ate dinner. By then, the pot roast had been reduced to a dry cinder, so they ate sandwiches on plates in front of the fire.

They talked a little, comparing their experiences growing up on a ranch, sharing tales of their respective travels, Tess's as the buyer for Maxwell and Danielson Imports, Jack's on the rodeo circuit. When their stomachs were finally full, however, they set their plates aside and simply sat, shoulders touching, and watched the fire.

Their easy, companionable silence made Jack feel more

than a little bewildered. He couldn't help but compare it to his marriage. Even during the first year, when he and Elise were still getting along occasionally, they'd never been able to just be together. Elise had craved talk, action and constant attention, and it hadn't taken long for him to resent it. They'd had sex, but that had pretty much been it. Once it was over, they'd gone their separate ways.

He looked over at Tess. She looked perfectly at ease with her long legs stretched out before her. She was naked except for his denim shirt. "What happened to your flannel?" he asked her.

"It's here somewhere," she said easily. "But I like this one better."

"Why?"

She leaned sideways and nuzzled his ear. "Because this one smells like you."

The simplicity of the answer caught at him. Without knowing what he intended, he turned to her. To his shock, he heard himself say, "Did you love him?"

Tess looked at him in surprise. "Who?"

"Nicki's father." He didn't know why it was so important all of a sudden—it simply was.

She met his gaze steadily. "Yes. He was my very best friend. I miss him every day."

"I see." Well, he'd asked. He had nobody but himself to blame for the sudden tightness in his gut. The tightness that he told himself wasn't jealousy.

Tess must have heard something in his voice, however. "It wasn't how it is with you and me," she said quietly. "There was no spark between Gray and I. We were friends," she said again.

"There must've been at least an ember," he said gruffly. "You have a daughter."

She linked her fingers with his. "We were together only

once. He'd just been diagnosed with the tumor, and we were both so devastated... Things got out of hand. But I don't regret it. Not for a moment. My only regret is that he died before I found out I was pregnant.''

Jack saw the tenderness blaze through her face as she spoke of the other man. For some reason, he had to look away.

''What about you?''

It took him a moment to change gears. When he realized what she was asking, he tensed. ''What about me?''

''Did you love your wife? At least at first?''

He shrugged. ''I suppose. It's not a subject I spend much time thinking about.'' He sent her a look meant to convey that the subject was closed.

She got the message and looked away. There was a long silence, one that wasn't as tranquil as those that had preceded it. Finally, she said, ''So. What did the weatherman say earlier?''

Gratefully, he latched on to the change in subject, feeling a little rueful when he realized he'd forgotten all about that piece of news. ''He said that it's finally going to warm up and the wind's going to stop.''

''Does that mean they'll come and plow the road?''

He nodded. ''We should be able to get out Friday at the latest.''

She was silent. ''Do you want me to go?'' she asked finally. ''There's no reason I can't stay in a motel until Gram gets back. You certainly don't have to put me up because of...this.''

His stomach flip-flopped. ''Is that what you want?''

She shook her head. ''No.''

''Then don't. The baby's settled here. Why upset her schedule now, when you'd just have to do it again when Mary gets back?''

For once, the emotion in Tess's dark eyes was impossible to read. "All right," she said slowly. "For the baby's sake...I'll stay." She stood abruptly and picked up their plates. "I'd still like to make a trip to town, though. Nicki should be seen by a doctor, and there are some other things I need to see about."

"*You* need to be seen by a doctor." He considered. "Things should be clear enough by the end of the week that we can make Gillette if we start early enough."

"Oh, no," Tess said matter-of-factly. "Gweneth will do just fine."

He stared at her, fighting to control his expression. The last place he wanted to take Tess was the town where Elise had spent the end of her pregnancy. The gossipmongers would have a field day. "Gillette's four times the size. And it's got more doctors."

"It's too far. Besides, I want to see Dr. Isaacs. He's still practicing, isn't he?"

"Yeah, but—"

"Good." Tess carried the plates to the counter. "That settles it, then."

Jack opened his mouth to disagree, then shut it. There was nothing to be gained by arguing. If they went anywhere, it was going to be Gillette. For her sake, that was all there was to it.

Tess strolled back toward the quilt. Jack's groin tightened at the sight of her long, bare legs. The knowledge that she was naked under his shirt didn't help matters.

She reached down and offered him her hand. "Come on. Let's go upstairs. It's been a long day."

He climbed to his feet. Sex was one thing. Sleeping together was something different, which he realized the second he thought about what it would be like to fall asleep and wake with her in his arms, to feel her softness against him all night long. He shook his head. "I don't think that's a good idea."

"Please?" If she'd begged or complained or tried to entice him, he might have stood firm. Instead, she simply stood there, looking at him. "I don't want to sleep without you," she said quietly.

She was close enough for him to note the change in her scent. Four hours ago, she'd smelled of herself and soap and baby powder. Now, she smelled like him—and the sweet, musky odor of sex. The scent went to his head like an exotic aphrodisiac.

Well, hell...why not? He wasn't foolish enough to think in terms of forever, but for now, for the space of the next few days, what could it hurt? "Okay."

Deep down, he knew it was a mistake.

He went anyway.

Nine

"So?" Jack opened the pickup's passenger door, his green eyes scrutinizing Tess as they stood in the miniature parking lot outside Dr. Isaacs's office. "What did he say?" He reached out to her and took the baby, lifting her in her new infant carrier with an effortless strength Tess envied.

She watched his expression soften as he glanced down at Nicki, whose little hands had started to wave in excitement the instant she heard his voice. Ducking his head, he leaned into the truck.

"He said you're three years overdue for your annual physical." She leaned forward to watch as he snapped the carrier into the base and began securing straps. "And that you ought to stop being such a stranger."

"Tess."

"He also said that Nicki is perfectly healthy and seems to be thriving. That he'd get the ball rolling on getting her a birth certificate. That I need to bring her back in two weeks for her first set of shots. And that you did such a good job delivering her, he's going to start giving out your name as an emergency midwife.''

"Terrific," Jack muttered. He took a step back and straightened, turning to confront her. "And what about you? Are you okay?''

She met his probing look with a slight smile. "I told you. I'm a fast healer.''

"Good.''

She felt a distinct thrill as his eyes got the heavy-lidded look she'd seen quite a bit of the past three days. "Yes." Her smile got a little wider. "It certainly is.''

He moved to one side and motioned her into the truck. She stepped forward and he gave her a boost onto the high seat, bending over to press a hot kiss to her mouth before he shut the door.

He was halfway around the hood of the truck before she caught her breath. She watched the weak sunshine glint off his dark hair and wondered if she'd ever understand him. She was starting to doubt it.

She knew darn well he hadn't wanted to come to Gweneth. He'd resisted the trip every step of the way, coming up with all sorts of elaborate reasons why Gillette was the superior choice, while refusing to explain his opposition to the smaller town. In the end, it had been that refusal that lost him the argument, since he couldn't dispute the fact that Gweneth was a good hour closer to the ranch and he wouldn't provide a reason why Tess shouldn't see Dr. Isaacs, who was an excellent doctor and had the added advantage of being someone she knew.

So here they were, although so far "they" meant her and Nicki, while Jack went his separate way. She'd told him she wanted to buy a car seat, and he'd dropped her in front of the general store and gone to gas the truck. When it was time to see the doctor, he'd walked her as far as the clinic door and said he had an appointment to see a man about a horse.

If not for that kiss, she might have thought he didn't want to be seen with her. Barring that, she was starting to think he didn't want to be seen, period.

It was a notion that gained credence as he climbed into the cab and gave her a sideways glance she couldn't interpret. "Doc say anything else?"

She shrugged. "Sure. We talked about his son Mike, who's a veterinarian in Cody. And about the mare you trained for his wife. We discussed Gram, and the ranch, and who's still around and who's not."

"Hmm." He fastened his seat belt, started the truck and pulled out of the parking lot. "I suppose he was surprised when he found out you were with me."

Tess glanced at him. His voice was too casual. "Maybe a little. At first. Then he seemed pleased. He said you'd had a bad time and deserved a little happiness."

He gave an elaborate shrug, but seemed to relax a fraction. "Nice of him."

"Maybe you'd like to elaborate?"

He shook his head. "Don't think so."

She swallowed a burst of frustration, but let the subject drop. She didn't want to have to pry information out of Jack; she wanted him to trust her enough to volunteer it.

She looked out at the town. They'd come only as far as the general store on the town outskirt's this morning, then backtracked to Dr. Isaacs's office, which was among the scattering of houses that made up the residential area.

"So?" Jack slowed the pickup to a stop at Gweneth's one and only traffic light. "Does it look the way you remember?"

She glanced around and nodded, taking in the string of

storefronts. The feed store was still the largest and most prosperous-looking establishment, not too surprising given that ranchers made up the bulk of the population for a hundred miles. The rest of the town consisted of a general store, a bank and a service station, a barbershop-beauty parlor, three taverns, two churches and two cafés, all located along the street that bisected the highway. "I guess so—except for the video store. That's new."

He shook his head. "They went out of business two years ago."

She smiled. "So where to next?"

"Home."

She turned to look at him. "Excuse me?"

He stared straight ahead, acting as if what he was proposing were the most normal thing in the world. "We got the car seat, you've been to the doctor's. What else is there to do?"

"Feed me, for one."

"We've still got all those sandwiches you made in case we got stuck. I thought we'd stop and eat at the rest area at Madeline Butte."

"Think again. I've been eating my own cooking for the past month. I want to go to Mabel's. Doc said she's still in business, and I dreamed about her chocolate cream pie the whole time I was pregnant." Tess didn't add that she wouldn't mind having a chance to show off Nicki, but there was that, too.

"We have to get started back," he said stubbornly.

She narrowed her eyes. "It's just past noon. It won't take that long to eat. Please?"

"No."

She sighed. "All right. But it's on your head."

He was silent a moment before he said reluctantly, "What is?"

"Doc says I'm slightly anemic." Desperate times called for desperate measures, and it was only a tiny lie.

"I thought you said you were fine."

"I am. I'm just supposed to eat on a regular basis. It's been a long time since breakfast, and we're forty minutes from Madeline Butte."

"So have a sandwich now."

"Eating in the car makes me nauseous." She had to bite her lip as the nerve in his jaw suddenly started to throb.

He took a deep breath, then released it. "Mabel's it is."

The light changed. He fed the truck gas and proceeded up the street. When they reached the café, which was fronted by half a dozen other pickups, he angled the truck into a parking slot.

Several people looked up as they entered, and a few of the men nodded to Jack as they made their way to one of the booths on the wall. A murmur of sound seemed to follow them, but it fell off as soon as they were seated. Tess told herself she'd imagined it.

And she might even have believed it, if not for Jack's obvious tension. He was so stiff, it was a miracle he could unbend enough to sit down.

Their waitress bustled up. She was a short, buxom woman in her fifties whose name tag read *Betty*. Tess had never seen her before, but it was obvious the woman knew Jack from her very first hello.

"Why, Mr. Sheridan," she said cheerfully. "I haven't seen you in a coon's age." Her eyes brimming with curiosity, she inspected Tess and the baby. "Now, who are these nice ladies?"

Tess waited for him to make introductions.

Instead, he stared at the menu and said, "Just friends," in a tone cold enough to freeze steam. "We'd like to order.

Two coffees to start, one decaf. Then I'll have the chicken-fried steak, and the lady will have…?"

"The cholesterol special, please," she said, rattling off the menu's name for the cheeseburger platter as she stared at him, shocked by his rudeness.

Only Betty seemed unfazed. She nodded, started to say something, then dashed off with a quick apology as a bell sounded in the kitchen and the cook yelled, "Order up!"

"Jack—"

He gave her a hard look. "Let it go, would you, Tess?"

Short of making a scene, she didn't know what else to do under the circumstances. She nodded.

The meal passed in almost total silence. By the time Betty returned to clear away their plates, Tess was actually glad to see her.

"You two want anything more?" the waitress asked.

"Yes," Tess said, in the same breath that Jack said, "No."

The waitress laughed. "So which is it, folks?"

"I'd like a piece of chocolate cream pie," Tess said firmly, shooting Jack a look that dared him to disagree. "And I wondered…is Mabel back in her office, by chance?"

Across the table, Jack's fingers threatened to snap the handle off his coffee cup.

"Nope. Today's her day off."

"Oh." She swallowed her disappointment, although she was relieved to see Jack's grip relax.

"That's sure a cute baby." The waitress took another long look at Nicki, then looked speculatively from Jack to Tess and back again. "You *sure* you two are just friends? 'Cause I gotta tell you, that little darling looks just like you, Mr. Sheridan."

Jack stared coolly back, his face impossible to read. "You're mistaken," he said stiffly.

"If you say so. I'll get your pie and be back in a jiffy."

Aware of Jack's strained expression, Tess ate her pie in a hurry. The second she was done, he tossed two tens on the table to cover the bill, picked up the baby in her carrier and stood. "Let's go."

Mystified and more than a little irritated by his behavior, she went willingly along to the truck, waiting until they were inside before she confronted him. "Okay. You want to tell me what that was all about?"

He shrugged and started the truck. "I don't like restaurants. Too many people."

"Is that it, really? Or are you just acting like this to pay me back for not agreeing to go to Gillette?"

"Hell, no."

"Then you won't mind if we make a quick trip to Marden's."

"Damn it, Tess—"

"Listen," she said reasonably. "I've got to have new underwear. Mine were in pretty sorry shape to begin with, and now that you've ripped that pair last night and—"

"All right," he said hastily. He backed out, drove down to the end of the street and did a U-turn, then came back up and parked on the other side of the street, in front of the town's clothing store. He set the emergency brake and turned off the engine. "Go on. I'll stay here with the baby. There's no reason to drag her along."

She looked at him, wishing with all her heart she had a clue what was going on.

"I shouldn't be much more than half an hour."

He gave her a long look, then nodded. "All right."

She started to reach for the door handle.

"Tess?" She turned to look at him, her eyes questioning.

He leaned over, slid his hand under her hair at the nape of her neck and tugged her toward him, holding her still for his mouth. Her breath caught. She could feel his heat, his hunger, his need. And, for a fanciful moment, a hint of desperation, which she quickly forgot beneath the suggestive thrust of his tongue. When he finally lifted his head, she felt as weak as a kitten. His green eyes gleamed with banked desire. "Don't take too long."

She cleared her throat. "I won't."

Her knees still weak, she climbed out of the cab.

Marden's Clothing Emporium hadn't changed at all in ten years, Tess thought with a sense of nostalgia. There was still the same curious hodgepodge of items, which ranged from a rack of chiffon prom dresses to an entire wall devoted to jeans in every imaginable size to a corner filled with accessories that ranged from rawhide roping gloves to satin hair bows.

Conscious of her limited time, she quickly grabbed a shopping cart. After a quick survey of the men's section, she picked out a few things for Nicki, unable to resist some little pink sleepers and drawstring nighties, a fuzzy hat, a well-insulated bunting and some fluffy booties. Then she grabbed two pair of jeans for herself, a pair of stretchy T-shirts and a dark purple sweater, some socks and a half-dozen pair of panties. Two new bras, by far the most time-consuming part of her shopping, since she had to try them on to find the right size, rounded out her selections—until she caught sight of a short, filmy black chemise. She grabbed that, too.

By the time she arrived at the cash register, she felt as though she'd run a marathon. In a way, she supposed she had; according to the clock above the cash register, only thirty-nine minutes had passed since she left Jack. She started piling things on the counter.

The clerk, a woman about Tess's age, rang up the first few items. "Hi," she said with a friendly smile. "Did you find everything you need?"

"Yes, thanks." Things had certainly changed, Tess thought philosophically. Just like the waitress, the clerk was a stranger. Once upon a time, she'd pretty much known everyone in Gweneth. Now, she didn't seem to know anyone.

"Are you new in town?"

"Not really. I grew up about seventy miles south of here."

The woman's fingers flew over the cash register keys as she worked her way through the pile of clothing. "It looks like you're here for more than a visit."

"Maybe. I'm Tess Danielson. My grandmother owns the Double D."

"Oh, I know Miss Mary. I'm Carole Marden."

Tess did a little mental juggling. "You must be…Jeff's wife? We went to high school together," she explained.

"How nice." She beamed. "We've been married eight years. His parents are retired, so now we run the store," she added unnecessarily.

The bell above the door rang, and they both turned to look as a pair of teenage girls burst in, talking and giggling excitedly. "Hey, Mrs. Marden," they chimed, sending two distracted waves in the older women's direction before they scurried over to stare covertly out the main display window. "I'm telling you, Elsa, that's him," the taller of the two, a plain, prim-looking redhead said in a carrying whisper. "I saw him last spring at the charity rodeo in Elmo. He rode in the cutting event. Whose baby do you suppose that is?"

"I don't know, but I bet it's not his," said her companion, a compact blonde. "My mama says it broke his heart when his wife up and left him, and them with a brand-new baby. That he's just pining away."

Tess followed the path of their gaze. Her chest constricted when she saw that the only person in sight was Jack. He was sitting in the truck, holding Nicki in the curve of his arm.

The redheaded girl shrugged. "Well, my mama says it's a disgrace the way he let that two-timing Jezebel have custody. She says there's not a judge in all of Wyoming who would have let her have that precious baby boy. Not after she left her husband for his very own brother."

"Well, I don't know about that," the blonde said uncertainly. "I feel sort of sorry for him. It must be hard having everyone in town know your wife cheated on you—"

The other girl gave an unattractive snort. "Mama says it's his own fault. That he must not have any backbone. That a real man would've kept what was his."

Tess stood, rooted to the spot, stunned by what she was hearing. It was suddenly very clear why Jack had been so reluctant to come into Gweneth. Her hands clenched into fists as she fought a very real desire to inform the redhead that her mama wouldn't know a real man if she found him naked in her bed.

Yet she knew that wouldn't help matters. Nor would it do anything to change the fact that it was Jack's *brother* who'd been—was?—the other man. She thought about how guarded and wary and alone Jack seemed at times. Now she knew why; the extent of the betrayal was staggering. *Oh, God. Oh, Jack. I'm sorry.*

She must have made some sound of distress, because Carole Marden suddenly spoke up sharply. "Girls! That's enough. I'm paying you to stock shelves, not gossip."

The two teens jerked around, as if only then realizing they could be overheard. "Yes, Mrs. Marden," they chorused. They turned slowly away from the window and headed for the back of the store.

Tess barely noticed. She was too busy trying to put what she'd just heard into some sort of perspective.

"I'm sorry you had to hear that." Carole began folding Tess's purchases and sliding them into bags. "But since you grew up around here, you must know how people love to gossip." She glanced in Jack's direction and clucked her tongue, a frown marring her pleasant features. "That poor, unfortunate man. It's just so sad…"

It took a moment for the woman's words to penetrate. Tess's head came up. "What did you say?"

"Oh, that it's just so sad how that poor man's life was ruined—"

Tess's eyes narrowed. It was bad enough that "Mama" seemed to blame Jack for his own misfortune, without having this stranger—no matter how well-intentioned—pity him. "Excuse me. But there's nothing sad or unfortunate about Jack Sheridan. And his life is certainly not ruined. Trust me." She dredged up a meaningful smile. "I'm in a position to know, since I live with him."

"Oh." The other woman's eyes widened. "Oh, but— I mean—" In the process of placing the last pair of Nicki's new booties in the bag, she suddenly appeared to make the connection between Tess's purchases and the pair out in the truck. "Oh, dear. I'm sorry. I didn't mean…"

There was a strained silence that Tess made no effort to ease. She took out her billfold. "How much do I owe you?"

The other woman turned her gaze to the register display with an air of relief. "It comes to $386.42."

There was a certain grim satisfaction to being able to pay

with cash. Tess handed over the money and collected her change. "Thanks. Tell Jeff I said hello."

"I—I will."

Her thoughts churning, Tess barely heard her as she hefted the bags and set off for the truck.

Tess was too quiet.

Jack glanced at her out of the corner of his eye. He'd known something was wrong the instant he saw her come out of Marden's. Everything from the set of her chin to the length of her stride had telegraphed her agitation. As had the way she jerked open the door, stuffed her trio of bags behind the seat and climbed stiffly onto the seat.

He'd braced for an explosion. But all she'd said was "I'd like to go home. *Now.*"

Except as related to the baby, she'd barely said a word since—and that had been close to an hour ago.

He put on the turn indicator and slowed the truck for the turn onto Johnson Number 9. Behind him, the weak winter sun was beginning to descend over the Bighorn Mountains, which stretched across the western horizon like a jagged curtain. In front and to each side, the terrain unrolled in an uneven sea of wind-scoured white.

Even with four-wheel drive, their trip on the county road this morning had been slow going, with four-foot drifts and patches of ice making for treacherous driving. Now, with dusk no more than an hour off and the temperature starting to drop, anything that had warmed today would be starting to refreeze.

It promised to be a hellish drive, demanding total concentration. And all he could do was think about Tess and wonder...if she knew.

Yeah, right. Do you really believe she's staring out the

window with that remote expression on her face because she's so enamored of the view?

His stomach twisted. All right. So what if she did know? What the hell did he care? It wasn't as if he needed her or something. He'd been doing just fine before she came into his life.

The only reason he was upset was because this probably meant no more sex. Which was pretty damn stupid. As far as he knew, there was no such thing as an uncomplicated sexual relationship. And even if there was, he and Tess were the last two people on earth to make it work. Neither of them had your garden-variety white-picket-fence sort of past. Both had their share of baggage.

Especially him.

So why don't you just admit it, Sheridan? Why don't you own up, at least to yourself, how you hate the thought of her knowing you weren't man enough to satisfy your wife? And that your own brother betrayed you? Or that you let your son go without a fight?

Well, that was pretty stupid, too. Hadn't he known that if she stuck around long enough she'd hear something? That it was just a matter of time? That there'd been a real risk in agreeing to go to Gweneth?

He sighed and tried to convince himself that this was probably best for them both, in the long run. It made sense to cut things off now, before there was any real involvement. She could go her way, and he'd go his, and—

"Jack?"

He was so absorbed, it took him a second to realize she'd spoken. He came to attention, surprised to find he'd been driving on automatic pilot and that they were already past the draw where Tess's car had been until he winched it out yesterday. "What?"

"Is the man your ex-wife's married to now...is he your brother?"

Even though he thought he was prepared, the direct question felt like a punch to the belly. His hands tightened on the steering wheel as he fought to get a grip on his emotions. "Who told you that?"

"No one. I overheard some people talking, saying the two of them had an affair, and I wondered. Is it true?"

He stared straight ahead. "Yes."

She released a long, pent-up breath. "Why didn't you tell me?"

"Why should I? It's not the sort of thing you brag about."

"But, Jack—"

"I don't want to talk about it."

"Really?" She stared at him in undisguised amazement. "Well, maybe I do."

"That's too damn bad, because you're out of luck. The discussion is closed."

She tried a different tack. "Do you have any idea the sort of things people are saying?"

He shrugged. "Sure. I just don't give a damn."

"Then why did you spend most of today sitting in this truck, doing your best to avoid the entire population of Gweneth?"

He was silent.

"Why, Jack?"

"It doesn't matter."

Out of the corner of his eye, he could see the pink in her cheeks getting a little deeper. "I guess that's good. Because that means you won't care that I told Carole Marden that we're living together, will you?"

"What?" He jerked around to look at her, and nearly

put the truck in the ditch. "Why the hell would you do that?"

"What was I supposed to do? She called you 'that poor, unfortunate man.' She said your life was ruined. It made me mad."

"Maybe you should have listened to her."

"Why should I do that?" she shot back. "It seems to me that there's already one person too many feeling sorry for you."

That cut it. She might not be done, but *he* was finished. He sent the truck shooting across the Cross Creek cattle guard. Up ahead, he could see the solid rise of the barn. All he had to do was hold on.

He hit the brakes and sent the truck fishtailing to a stop in front of the house. He slammed the transmission into park, switched off the ignition, shoved open the door and clambered out.

"Where do you think you're going?" Tess demanded.

"I've got chores."

"But—"

Disturbed by all the commotion, Nicki began to whimper.

"You'd better see to your daughter." He shut the door and walked away.

Tess told herself she didn't care that Jack had retreated to the barn. After all, a barn was the appropriate place for a man who was as blind as a bat, as stubborn as a mule, as pigheaded as a...pig. He could stay out there until the Fourth of July, for all that it mattered to her.

She repeated the sentiment regularly over the next three hours, muttering it as she put away her purchases, restating it as she fixed and ate a solitary dinner, reminding herself of it again as she bathed and fed the baby and put her to bed in a new pink sleeper.

She told herself the same thing as she stood in the dark and stared out the bedroom window at the barn.

The problem was, part of her didn't believe it.

It was the same part that kept remembering the hint of desperation in that kiss outside Marden's. And the way Jack's knuckles had turned white on the steering wheel when she asked that very first question about his brother and his ex-wife. And the stubborn way he'd refused to discuss anything.

If she didn't know better, she'd think he felt ashamed.

But why?

Oh, for heaven's sake, Tess. Think about it. How would you feel if it had happened to you?

She turned it over in her mind. She'd be hurt, of course. And she'd feel angry and betrayed and determined to never again make the same mistake.

And, she supposed, if the hurt went deep enough—as it would if you were cuckolded by your own sibling—she might start to wonder what was wrong with her, what she'd done to deserve such a fate. Particularly if her neighbors made it clear they were wondering the same thing.

It might very well be enough to make her shut down. To cut herself off from everyone and swear she didn't care...about anything.

And yet...what about the child? Try as she might, she couldn't square what she knew of Jack with a man who would voluntarily turn his back on his own child, no matter how battered he felt. Not when he was so tender with Nicki. And not when he'd been there for her, even when they were strangers...

She sighed, the last of her anger fading.

She no longer wondered if she loved him, she realized.

She knew. But her loving him wasn't going to do either of them any good if he wouldn't talk to her.

And as quickly as that, she knew what she had to do. She turned her back on the window and strode across the room to check on Nicki. Assured that the baby was fast asleep, she wasted no time, going swiftly along the hall and taking the stairs two at a time before she lost her nerve. She slipped on her boots and pulled on her coat in the mudroom, then plunged out into the night.

A full moon and a smudge of stars hung in the sky. While not nearly as frigid as it had been, it was still cold. She turned up her collar and stuffed her hands in her pockets, her feet crunching against the top layer of frozen snow.

She paused in front of the barn door to gather her courage.

Then she pulled it open and stepped inside.

Midway down the corridor, Jack jerked around to stare at her. He gave her a long, impenetrable look, then turned back and resumed rubbing the curry comb over Obsidian, who was loosely tied to an iron ring in the wall.

Tess took a deep breath and walked closer, moving to the gelding's head. The horse stretched out his nose to smell her. Recognizing her scent, he nudged her until she began to scratch his neck.

"I thought you'd be packed and gone by now," Jack said.

She looked over at him. Despite the chill, his coat was off, his shirt was unbuttoned, his sleeves were turned up. A light sheen of perspiration filmed his face and chest, while the muscles in his arms and back bunched as he worked the brush along the horses barrel. He didn't look at her.

Clearly, he wasn't going to make this easy.

"Are you throwing me out?" she asked.

He shrugged. "After today, why would you want to stay?"

She let the silence spin out before she answered, telling herself, as she had so many times before, that she had nothing to lose and everything to gain. Even so, her heart was pounding. "Because I love you."

The words momentarily froze him in midmotion. "You don't mean that." Although his voice was steady, the downward stroke of the currycomb jerked sideways.

Tess took it as an encouraging sign. "Yes, I do." She took a step toward him.

"No. You don't." He retreated around the back of the horse, came up the other side and jerked the lead line loose. He turned the gelding in such a way that Tess had to jump back to avoid being hit in the face by the horse's haunches.

She watched through narrowed eyes as he led the gray away into the far stall.

She waited.

He reappeared a few minutes later. His face impassive, he came down the corridor toward her.

When he was too close to easily avoid her, Tess stepped into his path. "Jack, listen. Please. I realize what you went through must have been awful. And I'm sorrier than I can say that two people you so obviously cared about betrayed you. But is it really worth ruining your life over?"

"You don't understand."

"Then explain it to me. Explain to me why you're so determined to be alone. Why you refuse to get on with your life. Why you've turned your back on your own child. Because I don't get it! Did you really love your ex-wife so much you can't let go?"

He recoiled. "Hell, no!"

"Then *what?*"

His face worked. "Isn't it enough for you that I wasn't

man enough to satisfy my wife? Or smart enough to know I was being deceived in my own house?"

"*No.*"

"Then try this on for size. *My son* isn't mine, and never was!" He stared at her, his expression hard with challenge. "Does that explain it?"

"Do you know that for sure?" Even as she asked, she knew the answer. Just as so many other things she hadn't understood now were clear.

"Oh, yeah. I've got the test results to prove it."

She squeezed her eyes shut. "I'm so sorry—"

"Save it. I don't want your pity."

Her eyes snapped open. "That isn't what I feel—"

He leaned forward so that they were standing toe-to-toe. "What I want is to be left the hell alone!"

"Well, that's too bad—because that's the one thing I can't do!"

"Why the hell not?"

He was so close she could see the dense green of his irises expand as his pupils contracted. It was like trying to stare down a tiger. There was a hint of danger in the air, a sense that one rash move might push him over the edge.

She looked steadily at him. "I told you. Because I love you."

Stubbornly he shook his head. "You don't mean that. You can't. Haven't you been listening—"

"Yes. You're the one who doesn't understand. It's over and done with. You didn't have a choice about what happened then, but you do have one about what happens now, about whether you put it behind you and get on with your life…or not."

"Damn it, Tess—"

She touched her fingertips to the seam of his lips. "You can swear all you want, but it's not going to change anything. So for now, why don't you just kiss me and make us both happy?''

With an explosive oath, he did just that. One second Tess was staring into his green eyes, and in the next she was in his arms, the cool wood of the tack room wall against her back, the solid strength of his hard length against her front, the drugging force of his mouth on hers.

A tangle of emotions rolled through her—relief, joy, tenderness. Fast on their heels came complete and total arousal as his lips slanted across hers again and again. She pressed against him, her pulse racing as heat spread through her core. It stole the strength from her arms and legs and consumed the air trapped in her lungs.

His tongue found hers. She felt faint, feverish, flushed.

She whimpered, wanting more. He complied, nudging her legs apart with his thighs until he was as close as he could be without being inside her.

An ache started low in her belly and concentrated downward. With a sob of need, she tangled her hands in his hair and nipped his bottom lip, trying to convey her growing urgency.

Jack groaned. He knew he should stop—but he didn't want to. Everything about her, her taste, her touch, the soft little sounds she was making deep in her throat, excited him. So did the way she was suddenly touching him, sliding her hands from his hair, down his neck, to the top of his shoulders. She trailed her fingers down his arms, then dragged his shirt out of his pants, echoing his sudden moan of satisfaction as she rubbed her palms over his hard belly. He wondered how much more he could stand as she explored the deep valley of his spine and the sleek flesh of his sides. He got his answer when she found his nipples. When she rubbed the pads of her fingers across them, he felt as if she'd touched him with a live wire. His entire body jerked with an overload of sensation.

He dragged his mouth away. Breathing hard, he rested his lips against her temple. "Tess...I can't— I want— You have to stop, or I'm going to take you right here..."

"For heaven's sake—*yes.*"

It was too much. She was the most unpredictable, exasperating, enticing woman he'd ever known—and he'd never wanted anyone so much. With a low, rumbling sound of need, he reached out, unsnapped her jeans and shoved them down, then did the same to his own.

He started to reach for her, but she held him off.

"Wait." Gripping his forearm for balance, she hastily toed off one boot and reached down to extricate her foot from her pant leg.

The sight of her long, smooth flanks and bare bottom destroyed the last scrap of his restraint. Unable to wait a second longer, he wrapped his arm around her waist as she straightened. He pulled her close.

She came to him without hesitation. Linking her arms around his neck, she lifted her face to his and rocked up on her toes in a provocative move that made his heart slam against his ribs.

He flexed his knees and thrust himself inside her, holding her gaze with his own. He saw her eyes widen, saw the pulse leap in her silky throat, saw the way her thick, russet-tipped lashes swept down. He heard her whisper of gratification, a long, breathless, "Oh."

"Look at me," he demanded, gritting his teeth for control as her wet, slick warmth closed around him.

She opened her eyes. Color rose in her cheeks as he established a steady rhythm. She rolled her hips, trying to make him hurry. He retaliated by manacling her wrists in his hands and raising them to the wall above her head.

The labored sound of their breathing filled the big barn.

Her lips parted, and one long leg climbed the back of his thigh, to hook around his waist to take him deeper. He felt her tense, saw the glazed look come into her eyes as her concentration turned inward, saw the moment when her head fell back. He reached down and slicked his thumb across the top of her wet, swollen folds, searching for the center of her desire.

She quivered. "Jack. Oh, don't, it's too much—"

He found it and pressed. For one long moment her body went rigid, and then her smooth, inner muscles clamped down. She shuddered and cried out, holding on to him as if he were her only link with the world.

Her pleasure triggered his own. Gripping her hips in his hands, he held her against the concentrated slamming of his hips. He felt the pressure build, so intense it was almost painful, and then the gushing rush of release as he poured himself into her, his entire body jerking with a sensation almost too exquisite to bear.

When he could think again, he realized Tess was still rocking him against her, gently stroking her hands down his spine.

He raised his head and looked at her.

Her mouth was wet from his kisses, her cheeks were flushed, her eyes were soft with satiation. Her expression soft and dreamy, she smiled at him. "Hi."

To his shock, he felt a tickle in his loins. "Tess. We shouldn't have—"

"Shh…" She stroked a hand through his damp hair, then leaned forward to press a kiss to his lips. "It was wonderful. Don't ruin it with regrets."

Jack tried to tell himself that she was right. But deep down, he was remembering all the things she'd said. And the vow he'd made never again to care too much.

And deep down, a part of him knew he was in trouble.

Ten

The soft murmur of Tess's voice woke Jack.

It took him a few moments to realize she wasn't in the bed with him. He rolled onto his side and found her standing at Nicki's cradle. Because it was dark in the big master bedroom, with only the faintest edge of gray framing the window shades, she was nothing more than a shadow against the night.

He propped himself up on one elbow. "Everything all right?"

"Uh-huh." Her voice was hushed. "I just finished feeding the little glutton here, and she's drifting off to sleep... aren't you, sweetie?" she said soothingly to the baby.

Jack laid his head back down on the pillow. There was something soothing about lying in the dark, listening to her talk to the baby. And about feeling included instead of excluded, for a change. A surprising sense of peace washed over him. For the first time, it didn't feel the least bit strange to find himself back in the same room and the same bed he'd once shared with Elise.

But then, nothing was the same as it had been. Not the room. Not the woman with whom he was sharing it.

And not him. He lay there, tested the unfamiliar emotion threading through him, and realized after a moment that it felt like...happiness. He still wasn't in the market for a long-term commitment, but for now...well, for now, this would do fine.

The mattress shifted as Tess climbed back into the bed. He reached out, pulled her close and stroked a hand down her back. He frowned at the goose bumps on her skin. "Cold?"

"A little. But you're not. You feel nice and warm." She nestled against him, and for a long space of time they simply lay there, both lost to their own private thoughts.

She stroked one slim, long-fingered hand across his chest. "Jack?"

"Hmm?"

"Tell me about them."

"Who?" he said, although he already knew.

"About...Elise and——?"

"Jared," he said finally, saying his brother's name out loud for the first time in more than three years. He waited for the familiar bitterness to surface. It didn't. To his surprise, all he felt was a curious sort of indifference.

Even more surprising was the discovery that he was finally ready to talk about what had happened—as long as it was to Tess.

He tried to decide where to begin. "Ever since we were little kids, Jared and I were best friends. I was two years older, the big brother, the serious one, while Jared...well, Jared could make folks smile just by walking into a room.

We rodeoed together. We double-dated. We dreamed about having a ranch.

"So we saved our money, and when we could afford it, we bought this place. At first, things were great. I worked my butt off. Jared charmed everybody in sight. Life was good.

"And then I met Elise at a cattle auction in Las Vegas. She was something. She sang in the chorus at one of the shows, and she was brash, sophisticated, wild. I'd never known anyone like her. I put off coming home for a week. We were married eight days after we met.

"Things started to go sour within a year. According to her, the ranch was too isolated, I worked too much, I didn't talk to her enough. I was always tired. I didn't take her to town. I wasn't *fun*. We fought—a lot—but I wasn't willing to give up. Instead, I asked Jared to help me out. To run interference. To keep her entertained."

He took a deep breath. "You would've thought I'd have caught on when she turned up pregnant, since by then our sex life had pretty much gone to hell. And I think I did know, deep down. I just didn't want to believe it. Not because of Elise, but because of Jared. So I acted as though nothing was wrong. I pretended not to notice the way he avoided me whenever he could, and wouldn't look me in the eye when he couldn't. I convinced myself it was normal for Elise to ask me to move out of our room and to want to go to Gweneth for her last trimester.

"When Matthew was born, I was the only one who was happy. I had my son. If I just held on, everything else would work out. And it did—for a few months. And then Jared and Elise came to me. They were sorry, they said, they'd never meant to hurt me, but they'd fallen in love and they were leaving."

Tess's arm tightened around him, and he found himself

groping for her hand. "They needed money, of course. And under the circumstances, they were willing to be reasonable—I didn't have to give Elise a penny, they'd settle for Jared's half share in the ranch," he said, unable to keep a trace of remembered bitterness out of his voice. "I said fine, anything, just as long as Matthew stayed with me...and that's when they told me the rest. I didn't believe them. God, I was angry. So we did the tests." Jack sighed, remembering. "The day after I got the results, I sold the entire herd to get them their money. And I told myself *never again.*"

Yet for some reason, he realized slowly, the wound didn't seem as raw now as it had been. As a matter of fact, it felt as if it had happened long ago, to somebody else....

Tess squeezed his hand. "I'm so sorry."

Her words jerked him back to the present. He heard the sincerity in her voice and found himself thinking that in some ways, they'd shared more in the past five weeks than some couples shared in a lifetime.

The thought was disturbing. As was the sudden memory of what she'd said to him out in the barn about it being time to make a choice. It occurred to him that now that he'd opened himself up a little, it would be natural for her to pick up the theme.

Only she didn't. Instead, as if she understood his sudden wariness, she shifted in his arms and came up on top of him. Robbed of his sight by the darkness, he was acutely aware of the way she felt against him—the firm mounds of her breasts pressed against his chest, the lithe strength of her thighs cradling his hips, the satiny slide of her sheath as she settled it against his sex.

He began to feel another sort of tension. "What do you think you're doing?"

"I'll give you a hint," she said softly. Slow and unhurried, she leaned down and began to kiss him. She paid homage to his temples, his eyes, his cheeks, his chin, before she settled her mouth over his with a sweetness that made him tremble. He raised his hands to touch her, but she caught them in her own and pressed them into the mattress on either side of his head. Then she began to explore him, sketching a line of kisses down his throat and along each shoulder. She lingered at the notch of his collarbone, at his nipples, at each shallow depression between his ribs.

She found his navel. She lingered there, too, and at the hollows that adjoined each hip, brushing her mouth over him, tickling him with the very tip of her tongue. She blazed a path to his thighs, rubbing her peach-soft cheeks against the long, hard muscles that were now rigid with his struggle for restraint.

And finally, when he was certain that he couldn't stand another second, she turned her attention to the rampant proof of his desire, rising full and thick to meet her. She kissed him there, too, with agonizing thoroughness, refusing to hurry, despite his heartfelt urging. Her mouth was wet, hot, hungry. She didn't relent until he'd gripped the mattress so hard he yanked the bottom sheet off the bed.

Only then did she move up his body, hold him steady, and fill herself with him. Bracing her hands on his chest, she began to ride him, slow and easy at first, then harder and faster.

Her technique didn't matter. Jack was lost from the first downward slide of her body over his. He wanted to make it last, wanted to guarantee her pleasure, but his control was gone. Breathing like a bellows, he surged upward, crying out as his climax struck him, so powerful that it made him feel as if he were being turned inside out. He was only vaguely aware of Tess calling his name as her completion was triggered by his.

Twined together, they held each other in the darkness. Jack felt Tess's heartbeat against his chest. A deep sense of possessiveness rolled over him.

At least for a while, she was his.

"Tess. Come here."

Tess frowned at the urgency in Jack's voice. Hastily adding the sleeper she was folding to the stack of clean laundry atop the kitchen table, she hurried over to the sink where he was bathing the baby.

"What's the matter?" She glanced curiously from him to Nicki, who was merrily splashing her arms and legs, secure in Jack's steady hands. Everything looked all right to her.

"Watch." Ignoring the water that soaked the front of his shirt, he leaned over. "Hey, little sweetheart," he crooned. "How're you doing?"

The baby went still, her expression growing sober as she focused all of her attention on him. She stared intently. And then her eyes lit up like the sun coming out, a brilliant smile curved her mouth, and she beamed at him.

It was impossible not to smile in response. And Tess did, although she wasn't sure exactly what the big deal was. After all, Nicki had been smiling for weeks.

She turned to ask Jack—and suddenly her heart stood still. To her astonishment, he, too, was smiling, his firm, chiseled lips curving in a way that took years off his face. She stared at him in amazement.

"What?" he demanded, the smile faltering as he saw her expression.

"Nothing. I just... That's the first time I've seen you smile."

"Oh." Now he looked mildly embarrassed. "Well, forget about that. You're supposed to be watching Nicki. She *smiled* at me," he added unnecessarily.

She regarded him for all of half a second before she reached up to give him a sympathetic pat on the shoulder. "I don't think so. Probably just gas."

He opened his mouth to object, then caught himself as she raised her eyebrows at him. Understanding dawned, and his expression turned sardonic. "Very funny."

Tenderness rippled through her. The last thing she wanted to do was embarrass him further, however, so she simply leaned forward, wiped a bead of water off the point of his chin and said lightly, "*I* thought so." As if nothing special had occurred, she walked calmly back over to the table and resumed folding clothes.

Inside, however, her heart was soaring. It had been a week since they made the trip to Gweneth, and with every day that passed, his guard seemed to come down a little more. Oh, he was still prickly and private and, despite what had just happened, not prone to wearing his heart on his sleeve. Yet some sort of internal barrier definitely had been breached. He was more open, more at ease, more willing to share his feelings.

She wanted to believe he was starting to let go of the past. That he was finally starting to look toward the future. Because she knew that they'd reached a crossroads of sorts. As much as she might wish otherwise, she couldn't will Jack to want a life with Nicki and her. It was a decision he had to make on his own, of his own free will. She'd made all the other moves in their relationship; now, it was up to him.

For that reason, over the past few days she'd come to a painful decision. When the time came for her to go, she would. No matter how hard it was, no matter how much it hurt, she would abide by his decision.

In the meantime, there would be no long faces for her. She meant to take each day as it came and savor every moment they had together. Losing Gray had taught her that life was too short to waste a second worrying about what you couldn't control.

Her gaze swung back to Jack like a compass seeking true north. She watched as he lifted the baby out of the water and laid her on a towel, talking in a low, confidential tone as he dried her off. With a deft touch that was astonishing, given the size of his hands, he diapered and dressed the little girl, then picked up a tiny yellow brush and styled her hair.

When he was done, he propped her up for Tess to see. "What do you think?"

She dragged her gaze away from him to glance at her daughter, and gasped. *"Jack!"* The baby's hair stood straight up in an outrageous rooster tail that made her look like a wide-eyed Woody Woodpecker.

"No?" Although his expression was solemn, there was a hint of a twinkle in his brilliant green eyes.

"No," she said with a laugh.

Chuckling, she rescued her daughter from him and took her upstairs to nurse before her nap.

When she came back down forty-five minutes later, Jack was still in the kitchen, talking on the phone in the kitchen. He turned at the sound of her footsteps. His expression was carefully blank.

"It's for you," he said quietly. "It's Mary."

Jack stared out the kitchen window, listening to the quiet murmur of Tess's voice as she talked to her grandmother. He wondered what was taking so long. His own conversation with the old lady had been blunt and to the point. She'd thanked him for his hospitality, while making it clear it was no longer needed. She wanted Tess and the baby at the Double D with her.

So? That was always the plan. How come you suddenly wish otherwise? Why do you suddenly want to rip the phone off the wall?

He rolled his shoulders, shying away from the answer. He told himself that his sudden sense of aggravation was simply resentment at having somebody else calling the shots. It had nothing at all do with Tess leaving.

So what if she did leave? They'd been thrown together by circumstance, they'd had their normal defenses stripped away by the extraordinary experience of birth, they'd made a mutual decision to explore their undeniable sexual chemistry.

It wasn't as if she were his wife or anything.

That's right. You care for her a lot more than you ever did Elise.

The realization froze him in place. He tried to deny it, but it refused to go away.

So ask her to stay.

Right. And then what? She might think ranch life was all right at the moment, but who knew how long that would last? She'd left once before. She could do it again.

Besides, she could do better than him. What did he have to offer except an empty house and a questionable future? And what about Nicki? She'd already lost one father. Under the circumstances, how could he ask Tess to stay, when he wouldn't—he couldn't—make any promises?

He took a deep breath as the decision was made.

The best thing he could do for everyone concerned was let her go. He looked over at her as she finally hung up the phone. "Well?"

Tess took in the grim look on Jack's face. Her heart felt unsteady, not because of her conversation with her grandmother—as challenging as it had been—but because of the decision that was surely coming.

She tried to keep her voice light. "Ten years doesn't seem to have mellowed her any. She says that my coming here without her consent proves I'm as 'precipitous as ever.' As does my 'blatant disregard for convention' in staying with you." At his questioning look, she shrugged. "Apparently she stopped in Gweneth on her way home and got an earful, thanks to my big mouth. She's willing to overlook all that, however, since I've had the good sense to provide her with a great-granddaughter. I've been commanded to pack my things and get myself to the Double D without delay." She tried to read his face and drew a blank. "All and all, I think it went pretty well." *Come on, Jack. Say something. Ask me to stay. Suggest I only go for a visit. Meet me halfway.*

"How soon do you want to leave?" he said woodenly.

The question was like a punch to the heart. She swallowed—hard—and told herself she was not going to make a scene that would only embarrass them both. Hadn't she told herself, promised herself, that she'd abide by his wishes? That whatever happened, it had to be what he wanted?

Yes. She'd gone into this with her eyes open. Jack had been honest with her from the start, had warned her not to expect anything. She ought to be glad this was happening now...while she still had a semblance of pride left and could take her leave with dignity.

It also didn't hurt that she felt more than a little numb, as if this were happening to somebody else.

She plastered a smile on her face. "The sooner the better, I think. If I start packing now, I'll be ready by the time Nicki wakes up."

He nodded, still wearing that same unreadable look. "I'll go put the infant seat in your car."

To her shock, he turned and walked out of the kitchen without another word. Tess stared after him, feeling as if she were suddenly caught in a bad dream. Everything seemed to be happening too fast. Only an hour ago they'd been joking and laughing, and now... *Now, it's over. Get a grip on yourself.*

It didn't take her long to gather her things; despite the shopping she'd done in Gweneth, neither she nor the baby had much. Of the items Jack had lent her, she kept, from necessity, a dozen diapers and the pale blue blanket with the rocking horse embroidered on the corner—and a single flannel shirt.

"Ready?"

She looked up. Jack stood in the doorway, as if he couldn't wait to get rid of her. He looked big and tall and as formidable as he had the first time she'd ever seen him. She could see nothing in his face. Not a hint of regret. Not a speck of affection.

She nodded and picked up the baby, watching as he came slowly into the bedroom and picked up her overnight bag and the suitcase he'd lent her.

Nicki was still fast asleep, but Tess cuddled her close anyway, needing the comforting contact, and stopped to take a final look around. She remembered that first night, how frightened she'd been, and how Jack had been there for her. She thought about how drastically her life had changed in the past weeks.

She took a deep breath and straightened her spine. Then she turned and walked out the door.

Eleven

Jack wasn't sure when he finally knew he'd made a mistake.

But he knew where he was when he got the first inkling. He was in the barn, where he'd gone to clean stalls after Tess left.

Added to his regular feeding and grooming tasks, the additional chore took him nearly four hours. Four hours in which to make countless trips past the spot where he and Tess had made love only days before. It was plenty of time to remember every detail of the passion they'd shared. To reflect on exactly what it was he'd given up. And to hear her clear, uncompromising voice in his head.

You didn't have a choice about what happened then. But you do have one now.

He tried to ignore it. But hour by hour, he started to wonder. Could it really be true? *Was* it his choice? But if it was, how could he be trusted to make the right decision about the future, when his choices in the past had been so disastrous?

Hell. He hadn't even had the brains to kiss Tess goodbye when she left, he thought tiredly as he switched off the barn's interior lights.

He stepped outside. To his surprise, night had fallen, taking the temperature with it. He shivered as the cold washed down his spin and clung to his sweat-damp body.

A smart man would have hurried toward the house.

But not him. He stayed where he was. If the barn was full of memories, the house would only be worse. Especially now, when it looked so dark and empty.

So? You've got nobody to blame but yourself. You knew better than to get involved. But you did it anyway, even though you knew better, and now you're paying the price.

There was always a price.

Only this time, it seemed inordinately high. And try as he might to convince himself that the reason for that was because he knew what to expect, knew down to the minute how long the days could stretch when there was no one to share them with, he didn't believe it. Not for a minute.

Because he didn't want just anyone, he admitted as he started along the path to the house, his feet dragging with every step. He wanted Tess.

The admission—as obvious as it was—knocked another hole in the shield he'd thrown up around his heart.

He let himself into the mudroom. Unmindful of the snow on his boots, he walked into the kitchen and switched on a light. He looked around at the cold, empty room. The folded laundry still sat on the table. The towels he'd used to dry Nicki after her bath still littered the counter. There was no fire in the fireplace, no food in the oven, no voice of welcome.

He tried to convince himself one last time that Tess's departure had been inevitable.

But suddenly, it just wouldn't wash. He could no longer deny that his stubborn refusal to ask her to stay was all tied up in that startling moment when he'd realized he cared for her more than Elise...or Jared...or even little Matthew.

He let out his breath and stood stock-still. *Come on. Admit it. Plain and simple, you panicked. You drove her away to save yourself from rejection. The same thing you've done to everyone the past three years.*

Only losing Tess was worse.

Because somehow, in just a matter of weeks, she'd made him care about life again. Because all of a sudden he *wanted*—her, Nicki, a future—more than he needed to hold on to the past.

Because...he loved her.

The realization rolled over him, knocking away the last of his defenses.

The only question was, what was he going to do about it *now*, when he'd already sent her away?

Tess looked out the Cadillac's windshield. Narrowing her eyes at the dazzling display of sunlight on snow, she decided—not for the first time—that she was probably crazy.

Why else would she be out at the crack of dawn, driving down a deserted county road in the middle of nowhere? After all, things had gone well at the Double D. After a little jockeying for position and some blunt talk, she and her grandmother had made their peace.

It had helped that they both agreed that Nicki was probably the most perfect baby ever made.

Yet Tess's heart had been heavy.

And, oddly enough, it had been Mary who put things in

perspective. Sitting in the big leather chair in her study, her great-grandchild secure on her lap, the old lady had looked over at Tess during a pause in their after-dinner conversation last night and said, "So? How long are you going to mope?"

"Excuse me?" As she'd noticed on the phone, time hadn't done a thing to soften her grandmother's blunt manner.

"Why'd you let that Sheridan fellow run you off, anyway? I thought I raised you better than that, Tessa. I thought I taught you to go after what you want."

Tess had narrowed her eyes at the old lady and told herself that Mary didn't know what she was talking about. And yet the idea had stuck. Is that what I'm doing? she'd wondered. Letting Jack run me off, because it's easier than fighting for what I want?

She'd denied it at the time, but sometime in the middle of the night she'd realized her grandmother was right—drat her. And that she was going to have to do something to remedy the situation.

So here she was, going back for one last try. Somehow, she was going to make Jack see that they were meant for each other. That he needed her and she needed him. And that life was too short to waste on regrets.

She was so lost in thought, she didn't see the steer until it was almost too late. Feet planted in the middle of the road, the beast looked as big as a bus.

Tess hit the brakes. Too hard. The Cadillac began to slide. As if it were moving in slow motion, the car glided slowly to the right, skidded gently along the verge for a hundred feet, then burst through the snow bank, bumped down the slope that edged the road and rolled to a stop.

She clutched the steering wheel. Well, heck, she thought

with a strong sense of déjà vu. Now what was she supposed to do?

She pondered her options—all one of them. There was nothing for it; she'd have to walk. With a disgusted sigh, she took a good look around. To her relief, the steer had finally hightailed it away, and could just be seen disappearing over the far hill. Shaking her head, she climbed out of the car, stuck her purse under the seat and locked the car up. Then she tramped up the slope onto the road. She brushed the loose snow off her boots and jeans. At least this time she was better dressed and in better shape for a hike, she reflected.

She had gone perhaps half a mile and was just starting to hit her stride when she heard the sound of a vehicle approaching. Shading her eyes with one gloved hand, she gave it a good look.

She stiffened. She recognized that pickup. It was Jack's.

She knew the instant he spotted her. The truck slowed, then sped up, then slowed again as it rolled to a stop in front of her.

Jack climbed out. A nervous flutter went through her stomach. On some level she realized he was dressed more formally then she'd ever seen him, in a good white shirt and a brocaded vest, black cords and a leather jacket. Yet mostly what she saw was the strain around his mouth, the way he had his hands closed loosely into fists, the way he hurried toward her as if he'd missed her as much as she'd missed him—

"Tess?" The sunglasses he was wearing didn't do a thing to camouflage his ferocious scowl. "What the hell are you doing out here?"

She stopped in her tracks. Yep, she was definitely crazy. Here she'd been making him into a needy romantic hero, while the truth was, he was as impossible as ever—and totally annoying. What on earth had she been thinking? That she'd waltz up to him, speak a few hard truths, tell him what a fool he was, and that he'd drop at her feet and make a passionate declaration of love?

Right. There was a better chance Nicki would get up from her nap and recite the soliloquy from *Hamlet.*

She lifted her chin. "I needed some fresh air and exercise," she lied.

He planted his hands on his narrow hips. "So you decided to go for a walk out in the middle of nowhere?"

"If you have to know, there was a steer in the road a mile or so back. I tried to avoid it and had a little accident."

There was a dead silence. His jaw worked with what she assumed was annoyance. "You going for a record or something?" he said finally. "Most encounters with a snowbank by an expectant or nursing mother in a single season?"

"Very funny. Are you going to give me a ride or not?"

"What do you think?" With the air of a man operating under a great restraint, he walked around to the pickup, opened up the passenger door and stood there, waiting. He was careful not to touch her as she climbed up, Tess noticed with a sinking heart.

"Fasten your seat belt," he ordered as he climbed in on his side.

She ignored him. What did she care about seat belts when her heart was breaking...again?

He waited.

Sighing, she complied. "Could we go now?"

He put the truck in gear. There was a silence that probably lasted a minute but felt more like an eternity. Finally, she couldn't stand it. She looked over at him, praying her heart wasn't in her eyes. "So...are you on your way to town?"

"No."

"Then how come you're out here, dressed like that, at this hour?"

He continued to stare straight ahead without saying anything for so long that she thought he hadn't heard her. And then, as he tightened his hands on the steering wheel, she realized he had.

She braced for him to tell her to mind her own business.

"If you have to know, I was coming to see you."

"Oh." It was all she could manage, since her heart seemed to be jammed in her throat.

"I've been thinking. About your dude ranch idea. And I thought...well, my place would work pretty well...if you're really serious. We work pretty well together, and I thought... I mean..." He cleared his throat. "The thing is, it would be good for everybody. You'd be close to your grandmother, and Nicki needs a father. Not that you couldn't do a good job raising her on your own, but I did help bring her into the world. In a way, that makes me responsible for her." When she still didn't say anything, his voice took on a desperate note. "I don't know if you've realized it yet, but that night in the barn, and then later...well, we didn't use any birth control. I know it may be too soon, and that you're nursing and all, but..." He trailed off. After a second, he glanced over at her. "Are you going to help me out here?"

She shook her head. "No."

His jaw bunched and he shifted his gaze forward again. "Well, what I'm trying to get you to see is that you ought to marry me, damn it."

"Jack?"

"What?

"Stop the truck."

Still looking straight ahead, he did as she asked. She unfastened her seat belt and scooted across the seat. When he turned to face her, she reached up and slid his sunglasses off. Her breath caught as she saw the jumble of emotions in his eyes. Hope, fear, uncertainty...*trust.*

"Say it," she said softly.

He looked at her, and it was as if she could see straight into his soul. "I love you, Tess. I love you more than I've ever loved anybody in my life, and I want you to be my wife."

She blinked against a sudden rush of tears. "Oh, Jack. I love you, too."

"Is that a yes?"

"Yes."

"Thank God." The words were a prayer and a celebration. He pulled her into his arms. For a long space of time, he just held her, as if afraid to let her go. And then his mouth found hers and he kissed her, long and sweet, with nothing held back.

Tess realized it was his promise for their future.

Happiness filled her. She smiled as his mouth lifted from hers. He smiled back, and she suddenly knew that whatever happened, they'd get through it.

He rested his forehead against hers. "So how did it go with Mary?"

"Fine." She leaned against him. "She's every bit as impossible as she ever was."

"Then how about we go rescue our daughter? I miss her. And I'm ready to go home."

Together, they did just that.

*   *   *   *   *

And the Winner Is...
You!

...when you pick up these great titles
from our new promotion at your
favorite retail outlet this June!

Diana Palmer
The Case of the Mesmerizing Boss

Betty Neels
The Convenient Wife

Annette Broadrick
Irresistible

Emma Darcy
A Wedding to Remember

Rachel Lee
Lost Warriors

Marie Ferrarella
Father Goose

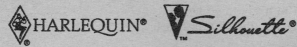

New York Times Bestselling Author

REBECCA BRANDEWYNE

FOR GOOD OR FOR EVIL—
THE INSIDE STORY...

The noble Hampton family, with its legacy of sin and
scandal, suffers the ultimate tragedy: the ruthless murder
of one of its own.

There are only two people who can unravel the case—

JAKE SERINGO is the cynical cop who grew up on the
mean streets of life;

CLAIRE CONNELLY is the beautiful but aloof broadcast
journalist.

They'd parted years ago on explosive terms—now they
are on the trail of a bizarre and shocking family secret
that could topple a dynasty.

GLORY SEEKERS

The search begins at your favorite
retail outlet in June 1997.

 **MIRA** The brightest star in women's fiction